I
CHOOSE
YOU

Aderonke Moyinlorun

AdomPublishers

Illinois. Indiana

Copyright © 2014 by Aderonke Moyinlorun
ISBN-13: 978-0615960876
ISBN-10: 0615960871
First Printing, 2014

AdomPublishers
Indianapolis,
IN46224
Tel: 812-233-3638

This edition is printed and bound in the United States of America by Createspace, Charleston SC.

To the most amazing woman in my life.
Mom, this book is all yours. . .with love.

ONE

Tamara had just received the news that Raymond tested positive for arsenic poisoning in his hair samples. And even though the doctor said the poison wasn't yet chronic and could be treated, she still felt as if Raymond had received a death sentence. She had called his cellphone and told him she needed to see him immediately.

When she heard the doorbell ring, she ran to the door.

As she set her eyes on Raymond, relief coursed through her. Raymond was still alive. He wasn't dead yet. And she wouldn't be able to live if he died.

With a sob, she flew into his arms and kissed him, moaning with pleasure as his arms enfolded her.

After a few seconds, Raymond broke the kiss and pulled away. Holding her upper arms, he studied her, looking her straight in the eyes. "Mara, are you okay?"

She shook her head. "I don't want to lose you. Not now. Not ever."

His surprise was obvious, but he bent down and gave her a melting kiss that pulled the pieces of her heart back together.

Desire and need overcame her, and she pulled him toward the couch, bringing him down on top of her. "I love you," she whispered.

His eyes grew hungry. "I love you, too, Mara. I love you too too much," he whispered as he pulled his woman lovingly into his arms.

Raymond moaned lustfully into their passionate kiss. He pushed her onto the brown leather couch, enjoying the sensation of her long, smooth legs wrapping around his waist.

Just a day ago, this same woman had told him they were over. But he knew they could never be over. He couldn't imagine life without her.

As he stared down at her perfect body, he forgot everything about her ultimatum "Choose me or we're over," she had demanded. Nothing was worth being without her, even for a moment.

Tamara yelped slightly as her head met the cushion, surprised by how he was taking her. Not that she was complaining as his fingers fumbled over the buttons on her blouse, working vigorously to free her of its constraint. She silently cursed herself for deciding on this shirt.

Raymond felt her long, nimble fingers slip into his black denim jeans, gently stroking him, making the task of removing her shirt almost impossible. He bit down on her bottom lip, trying to contain his ecstasy and failing miserably as a groan escaped his mouth.

Ripped free from her cotton shackles, Tamara

felt Raymond's lips trail down her neck, ever so often, nipping at the sensitive skin at her nape. She let out a deep moan, the fire within her beginning to blaze. It hungered for him. He could never be too close to her.

She was so caught up in the feel of his lips against her skin that she barely registered him removing her lingerie, but when he entered her, she let out a high-pitched whine of surprise and pleasure.

Her keening only fueled Raymond's desire. Her slick heat pulsated, tightening around him with every thrust. It was addictive and terrifyingly perfect. Her fingers, now clutching his back, clawed at his skin, drawing him into her further, wanting so desperately for his touch. The pain shot through him, somewhere becoming pleasure, as the world melted around him. His eyes shut tight, his ears filled with the fierce panting of the woman beneath him, his name being spoken, broken only by the moans of pure delight that held Tamara in its grip.

His orgasm shot through him, white hot and burning with frozen intensity that he had never felt in past encounters. She matched him, her mewling reduced to sputtered cries as her nails dug deep into his skin.

Tamara gulped for the air that had been ripped from her lungs, her dark hair plastered to her forehead and sweat beading down her skin. She turned ever so infinitesimally, unwrapping her legs from around him, allowing Raymond to lie next to her as he collapsed.

Raymond let a small smirk run across his face.

Yes, the sex had been short and fantastic, but there was something more to this type of intimacy.

It proved that no matter how many times Tamara tried to end things with him, they were never going to be over. They belonged with each other.

His strong, muscled arms pulled her closer. "You wanted us to talk?" he asked in a whisper.

As they tried to squeeze themselves to fit on the couch, she lay on her side and faced him, their bodies knitted together. "So does this mean we're not over? That I'm something more than your mistress?"

"You've always been more than a mistress, and you know that. But..."

She pulled away a little. "But what?"

"But for me to declare us to the world right now would be difficult, and it will complicate so many things."

Tamara pulled away and sat up on the couch. A million emotions clashed through her. She felt... she didn't know what she was supposed to be feeling right now. Anger. Disappointment. Disgust. Hurt. She felt hurt, but then lately, she had been hurt so much that she was getting used to the feeling.

For one long second, as she sat next to him on the couch, she said nothing. She suddenly felt the need to cover her nakedness, but she didn't, reminding herself that he was the same man who had made love to her moments ago.

Finally, she was able to speak. "What are you trying to say? I don't quite follow."

He brushed a strand of damp hair away from her face and behind her ear. "What I'm trying to say is that my heart already chose you. You didn't have to ask me to choose you."

"I'm not in the mood for fairytales. Don't throw sweet words at me. Let me understand what you're trying to say." Her voice was harsher than she had intended, but that didn't matter.

Raymond let out a sigh and then slowly sat up. He grabbed his t-shirt and gave it to her. "Put it on and let's talk. I know you felt like getting dressed seconds ago."

Tamara glanced skeptically at him. "So now you can read my mind?"

"No, but I know you. I know you a lot more than you know."

Tamara withdrew her skeptical look and quickly put on the shirt. The size of the t-shirt made her look awkwardly small.

After she put on his shirt, she waited for him to speak. Raymond drew closer and held her palms in his hand. His palm was large and made hers seemed so small. Looking into her eyes, he began, "When I said my heart chose you, I wasn't just throwing sweet words at you. I mean it." He was quiet for a short while, thinking about the best way to say what he wanted to say without hurting her feelings. "When you told me to choose you or else we'd be over, I thought you wanted me to go public with our relationship. Am I right?"

Tamara gave a weak nod.

"I thought about it. Trust me, Mara, I want to go public with us. I want you to be my wife. I want to marry you in a big fairytale wedding like you dream of. But we have to keep things low for now. There's too much at stake. I'm worried about you, about your job. You will lose a lot of clients. Your career will be destroyed!"

She cut him off. "And I told you I'm willing to give it all up for you!"

"And I believe you. Absolutely. But did you believe me when I said I know you a lot more than you think I do?"

Tamara watched his eyes, trying desperately to know what he was getting at. When she couldn't, she nodded gently. "I believe you."

"Good. That means you'd believe me if I say that you want to give up your career for me because that's the way you feel right now. What about in the future when you feel your life needs a purpose? When you feel the need to help people, but you can't get your career back because you married your client's husband?"

She pulled her brows together in a frown. "Are you saying that my feelings for you will change in the future?" She released her hands from his hold. "I know what I feel, okay? And my feelings for you will never change. Never!"

Raymond swallowed hard. "And I believe you, but if you know that you're imperfect, and that I have many flaws, too. And one day I might not be the best husband, and I may not be available, and you might want to take comfort with your job, you will agree with me on this. You're a career woman, and I'm not complaining. I love you like that, just the way you are. Your job and I are the two things you love most in this world, and I'm not about to take any of it away from you. Putting your career on the line for us is too much. It's like putting the very essence of your life on the line, and no one should have to sacrifice that much."

He moved to reclaim her hands. He held them tightly in his, watching her almost wet eyes intently. "I know you love me so much that you can sacrifice anything for me, and I the same for you. But you love your job, too. And I'm not going to take any of it away from you. You can have it both ways. You can have it all. It's my job to make sure of that. So, please, Mara, all I ask for is a little time to figure something out. I will find a way, I promise. A little more time is all I ask for."

As stupid and unreasonable as it seemed, Tamara didn't want to understand that he was looking out for her. A part of her was saying that this man was playing her, using her and toying with her. And that part was hurting deeply. The other half of her was telling her to trust Ray; that he'd find a way for them to be together. She was so conflicted that she didn't know how to respond. The two parts brawled inside her, until the one that was hurting won.

Ever so slowly, she released her hands from Raymond and glanced away. "I stole your shaving razor..."

"Don't change the subject, Mara! You've got to let me know if you agree with me on this."

Tamara continued in the same pace. "I stole your shaving razor and sent it in for a toxin test."

"You did what? I told you to stay away from

this, didn't I?"

Tamara glared at him. "Do you have a death wish?" she yelled. "Because guess what? It's coming true. You tested positive for arsenic poisoning!"

The room went dead silent for a minute. Tamara didn't want to break the news like that, but he'd given her no choice.

Her voice went back to being gentle. "The doctor said it's minor. You can still get treated."

"This is not about getting treated," he replied, his voice husky from the lumps building up in his throat. "We have to know the source. It could have been environmental. Or someone might be feeding me with it. Whichever, we need to know."

"Well, I can't think of any other way you got poisoned except that your wife is feeding you with it."

Raymond shook his head. "No, it can't be Dahlia."

"Look, I get the fact that Dahlia is your wife and the mother of your son, but that shouldn't blind you from seeing how evil she can be."

"Trust me, I know what Dahlia is capable of. She might be evil, but not that evil."

"She told me that she was going to kill you!"

"Sometimes we threaten to do things we can't do."

"What are you trying to say?"

"I'm saying we should widen our suspicions. I'm not totally ruling out the possibility that Dahlia could do it, but when you're a billionaire, a lot of people want you dead. Most of the board of directors are not happy with me. You don't think any of them could want me dead? Someone makes my coffee in the office every day—you don't think that person could be feeding me with arsenic? And your friend, Drake Johnson, has loved you since the beginning of time, and you don't think he could want me dead for getting in his way?"

Tamara's caution flared. "Drake is not capable of such a thing! He can't kill anyone!"

"You'd be surprised to know what love makes people do."

"Drake is a good person. I've known him longer than most. There are only a few good guys out there, and Drake is one of them."

"I'm not saying he wants to kill me. I'm saying that there are a lot of people out there who stand to gain something if I die. We should be looking at other possibilities and…"

Tamara cut him off. "How do you know Drake had feelings for me? I mean, I didn't even know that until recently?"

"You didn't know? It was so obvious. I think you're a very smart lady, but I'm beginning to doubt that."

"This has nothing to do with whether I'm smart or not. I was so in love with you that I couldn't see any other man…"

"Did you say you were in love with me?" Raymond asked. "You used 'was' for us." It sounded as if they were no longer in love. "Does that mean you're still insisting we're over?"

Tamara didn't respond.

"I thought you understood. I thought we were back together. We just made love, didn't we?"

Tamara shook her head. "That sex we had, it meant nothing. The doctor told me you tested positive for arsenic. I was scared. The sex was a thank-goodness-you're-still-alive kind of sex."

Raymond nodded with a sarcastic smile. "Thank-goodness-you're-still-alive kind of sex," he repeated. "I didn't know there was a type of sex like that. My teacher didn't mention that in my Sex 101 class."

"Ray!" she yelled to stop his sarcasm.

"What?"

She rose from the couch and walked toward her bedroom. "Goodnight, Mr. Connor. See you around."

"So now I'm Mr. Connor? Not Ray, not baby or sweetie."

"Why should I call grown-ass man 'baby?'"

"Because I'm your baby."

"Go home, Mr. Connor. Make sure to shut my door when you leave."

"Well, you have my shirt," he said, raising his voice loud enough for her to hear him.

"Go home, Ray! Goodnight!"

Raymond sank back into the couch, the news hitting back at him. He was trying to lighten the mood, but the imminence of death scared him to the bone. He shivered at the thought of it. If he died, Mara wouldn't be able to move on without him. If he died…

He shut his eyes, swallowed and said in his heart, "God, please, if anything happens to me, please ease her grief." He meant it more than any prayer he had ever said.

Slowly, he stood up from the couch, walked to the bedroom and gently slipped into bed beside Mara.

"I thought I told you to leave," she whispered.

He pressed closer to her and held her in his arms. "Mara, please, not this night."

"Ray!" she said, her voice a hardened whisper.

"Life is short, Mara," he replied. He sounded as if he was hurting. "These could be my last days, and I want each second I spend with you to matter. So, just say nothing and lay in my arms till morning. Am I asking for too much?"

Tamara didn't respond. She just lay quietly in his arms and listened to the beat of his heart. Each beat reminded her that this heart that beat for her could stop any minute.

TWO

The next morning, after breakfast, Tamara reached a decision, and it was time to let Raymond know about it. As they stood in the living room, she folded her arms across her chest and glanced at him. "What are your plans?" she asked.

"What plans?"

"Do you want to go to the hospital and get treated? You want to inform the police about this and let them do their jobs or…"

He cut her off. "I'm going to the hospital, but, no, we're not involving the police."

She drew back slightly. "Why?"

Raymond breathed out and put his palm on his forehead. "Mara, please stop!"

"Why don't you want to get the police involved?" Tamara asked again.

"Because I don't want history to repeat itself!" he replied, almost yelling.

"What? What history?"

"Mara, please, not now."

She walked closer to him. "What history, Ray?"

"I'll see you later," he said, giving her a quick

hug and walking speedily toward the door.

"I have an answer for you," Tamara said, raising her voice.

He halted. "What?"

"Last night, you asked if I understood the reason you can't choose me. I have an answer now."

He took a deep breath. "You know the right words to say to stop me." He turned to face her. "What is your decision?"

Tamara took a few steps closer to him. Looking straight into his eyes, she swallowed hard and began. "I get it. You love me, but you don't want me to sacrifice my career for us. I get it, but I don't understand. Meaning I'm still standing my ground — we're over until you do the right thing. I don't want to be a mistress... but I want to help you get through this."

Raymond scowled. "I don't need your help."

"Yes, you do. You asked for more time to figure out a way for us to be together. So while you're doing that, let me use that time to help you. It's a win-win. Although we're taking a break from our relationship right now..."

"Break? A break?"

"Yes! We're taking time off. You can use that time to figure out a way for us to be together, and I can use that time to save you and find out who is doing this to you."

"Mara!"

Moving closer, she locked eyes with him. "I'm not asking. This is what I want. And it's your job to give me everything I want, right?"

"Don't play that card, Mara. I said it's my job to

give you everything, but not something like this. Especially not when you're asking for 'time off'.'" He emphasized 'time off.'

Tamara gave him a sarcastic smile. "I'm going to assume that it's a yes. So, this is what I want. You're my client, so you're going home right now and you're going to pretend that you did not just hear the news of your own death. You're going to act normal and prepare for work. Before you actually go to work, you will meet me at Dr. Morgan's hospital..."

"Why..?"

She cut him off. "Because I trust him. So go home right now, and I'll see you at the hospital in thirty minutes."

"Thirty minutes?"

"Not enough? Okay, see you in thirty-one minutes."

He smiled, warm and vibrant. "Mara," he said gently as his gaze slid down her face and over the rest of her body, "you won't stop fascinating me." He moved to place a small kiss on her lips, but before he could, Tamara drew back slightly.

"WOW! So now I don't get a kiss?"

"You want a kiss?" She moved closer to him. Arms around his neck, she drew his face down and gave him a quick, light kiss on both cheeks. "That's all you get."

"Seriously?"

She gave another sarcastic smile. "Bye, Mr. Connor." She pushed him toward the door. "See you later."

Raymond smiled back. "See you."

Immediately after he got out of the room, Tamara placed a quick phone call. "Hello, Drake," she said.

"Hello, Tamara. You refuse to date me, and you refuse to stop chasing me. Make up your mind, girl."

"I am not chasing you! I'm your boss, remember?"

"Really? I think I forgot that for...."

She cut him off. "Drake, I want you to get me any information on Rachel Brock."

"Rachel Brock? That's Raymond's mom. Why are we digging up on her?"

"Raymond and I were talking about Dahlia, and he said he doesn't want history to repeat itself. I can only think it has something to do with his mom."

"So ask him about it. Wait! You said 'Raymond and I were talking.' Does that mean you got back together again?"

Tamara smiled. "Not exactly. And..."

"C'mon, you can talk to me. What's up?"

"About last night, Drake. You said you love me. I don't think it's appropriate to talk to you about my relationship..."

"Beep! Beep! Thank you for calling Drake Johnson. I'm not available to answer your call right now. Leave me a detailed message, and I'll get back to you. Bye!"

"Drake!"

He hung up.

****

Raymond had just parked in the garage and gotten out of his car when he saw Joe Connor walking out from his front door. "Hey, bro, what's up? It's kinda too early to be here," Raymond said.

"Business. I dropped by to talk to you before we went to work, but obviously my married brother does not spend his nights at home."

Raymond playfully slapped his shoulder. "Hey, don't crucify a brother." He smiled and pointed back to the house. "Come on, let's go inside."

They began to walk to the house, but before they could open the front door, Raymond caught Joe staring at him. "Okay. Joe, what's wrong? When you look at me like that, something is wrong."

"You tell me. What's going on with you, Ray?" Worry took over his once relaxed face. "Have you seen yourself in the mirror lately? You look like death. What the hell is going on here?"

Raymond laughed. "You've seen death before? What does death look like?"

Joe frowned. "Dammit, brother! Everything is not a joke!" he yelled.

For the next few seconds, no one said a thing. Finally Joe broke the silence. "I'm sorry. I shouldn't have yelled..."

Raymond cut him off. "It's okay. I really need to start taking things more seriously. We need to have a long talk."

Raymond opened the front door, and they both walked in. Joe sat on the couch, waiting patiently to hear what Raymond had to say.

Raymond sat next to him on the couch. Without looking at his brother, he began, "I've been sick."

"Since when?" Joe asked.

"One or two months ago. I'm not sure. It started as a harmless stomach problem. I talked to my doctor. He ran several tests, but he couldn't find out what was wrong with me. In the end, he gave me a pain reliever to deal with the pains in my stomach."

"So this thing is killing you, and you don't know what it is!"

"Tamara is taking me to see another doctor today. The doctor thinks I might be suffering from some kind of food poisoning. Cyanide or arsenic, I forget which one. Hopefully, this doctor can cure me. If not…"

"If not, then what? You're just going to give up?" He shifted closer to him. "Ray, health is wealth. "You can get the best doctor in the world just to save your life. We can afford it!"

Raymond smiled painfully. "Squander all the Connor wealth on medical bills while I let my family suffer?" He shook his head. "No, thanks."

"Well, that's noble of you! But you know what Dad would have done?"

Raymond shook his head.

"Dad would have invited the best doctors from all over the world. You may possess his business skills, but this trait of wishing to die so badly you didn't get that from him. Dad always wanted to live, no matter what!"

"And yet HE DIED!" Anger flared in Raymond's eyes. "What? You think I don't want to live? Do you know how many doctors I've visited in the last two months? Do you know how many needles have been stuck through my skin to draw blood for endless tests that yielded no results? You think I don't want to live?"

"Ray!"

"Do you know how many pills I have to swallow every morning just to stay healthy? Just to live a little longer? I've accepted it, but I'm still trying. Maybe I'm not trying as hard as Dad would have, but I'm trying to spend my last days in happiness like Dad. When he was about to die, he reconciled with me, and…"

Joe cut him off and completed his statement. "He took his last breath in the arms of the son he loved so dearly."

Raymond nodded. "And I'm doing the same thing, too."

"That's why you reconciled with Tamara. You didn't just walk into her office to ask her to be your divorce attorney. You wanted her to be in your life so that you can take your last breath in the arms of the one you truly love. You wanted her forgiveness. You wanted her love and to reconcile with her before you die."

Raymond nodded gently. "Asking her to be my divorce attorney was just an excuse to see her and to get back into her life."

"You've been preparing to die," Joe said. Tears filled his eyes, and he quickly buried his face in his palm. "My own brother has been living in pain, and I didn't even see it."

Raymond held him. "Hey, buddy, you can't crash down on me now. I'm going to need you to be strong," he said, patting his shoulder.

Joe held back the tears and looked at Raymond. "I'm strong."

"Raymond nodded and gave a painful smile. Still holding his brother's shoulder, he continued. "And that's why I'm going to need you to do a lot of things if I die. You're going to take care of Connor Corp. You're going to take care of Dahlia and my son. And most importantly, you're going to tell Mara that I wanted her to move on without me."

Joe nodded.

"Good. Now, you have to let me go. Mara will kill me. I'm running late for this doctor's appointment."

THREE

"You're late!" Tamara yelled as Raymond walked over to her. "I've been waiting for an hour. I hate waiting."

"Ouch! Painful!"

Tamara ignored his sarcasm. "Is that all you're going to say?"

"What do you want me to say?" Raymond said, smiling.

"Sorry, for a start."

"You're not getting one."

She glared at him.

"What? It's payback for when I waited two hours for you in your office and you didn't even apologize when you finally came in."

"Oh! So this is payback time, huh?" Tamara asked.

He shrugged. "Well, we're taking time off, right? It might as well be payback time."

"Maybe I should screw and marry your brother as a payback for screwing and marrying my best friend."

"Mara!" he said, his expression turning serious.

She had already said it and wished she could take it back. Silence suffocated them for a minute. "I've forgiven you, but we're not yet at that point where we can joke about it. I know that now."

Raymond nodded. "Can we go see the doctor?"

"Of course."

Opening the door, Tamara and Raymond walked into the doctor's office.

"Hello, Dr. Morgan," Tamara said as she walked into the office.

Dr. Morgan stood up from his armchair, arms wide open, as he gave a big smile. "Tamara, long time no see."

She walked speedily into his arms. "I know. I've missed your boring jokes."

"I've missed your long sermons, your ten commandments—Love your wife to pieces. Create time for your wife. Never hit your wife. Never give your wife a reason to want another man. Do not lie. Tell the truth, but be prepared for the consequence, some truth will ruin marriages..."

Tamara cut him off. "Okay, you still remember, but it's not enough to remember. You have to practice it."

"Every day," he replied. "How do you think I've been able to stay married to Lucy?"

Tamara smiled. "By practicing the ten commandments," she replied.

Raymond cleared his throat to remind them that he was standing there.

"Oh! Dr. Morgan, meet Raymond Connor." She turned to Raymond. "Raymond, meet Dr. Morgan."

Raymond extended a hand in greeting. "Hello, Dr. Morgan. Nice to meet you."

Dr. Morgan took his hand in his. "Nice to meet you, too, Mr. Connor. I've heard quite a lot about you."

Raymond smiled. "I hope they're all good things."

Dr. Morgan didn't respond. He gently let go of Raymond's hand, gave him a long, scrutinizing look, and then turned his gaze back to Tamara. "He's the one suffering from arsenic poisoning?" It was more of a question than a comment.

Tamara looked back and forth from Raymond to Dr. Morgan. "Yes, he is. I didn't tell you. How did you know?"

"Because I'm good at what I do," he replied, and then looked back at Raymond. "You're pale, tired, weak and dehydrated. In the last few minutes, you've touched your stomach more than ten times and winced. That tells me you might have abdominal pain. Your fingers are discolored, and you've got Mees lines in your fingernails. And I could go on if you want me to, but I'll stop."

Tamara sat down in the armchair and gestured to Raymond to take a seat. "You're right, Dr. Morgan. But you told me the poisoning could be treated by some kind of therapy or…."

"Yes. It's called chelation therapy. It's a method used for removing poisonous heavy metals from the body. In your case," Dr. Morgan said, looking at Raymond, "arsenic. Are you allergic to peanuts?"

He shook his head. "No."

"Good," he replied, taking a paper off the stack on his table and writing on it. "I'm going to put you on Dimercaprol, frequent doses at 3- to 4-hour intervals for several days. We are going to keep you here and watch you in case there are any side effects. And I'm going to have to inform the appropriate authority so that your environment can be monitored and cleaned of any poisonous substances. You know, to prevent others from getting exposed to this kind of deadly substance…"

Raymond cut him off. "I can come in every morning to take my treatments, but you can't keep me here. And you can't inform the authorities about this…"

Dr. Morgan went quiet for a second, shifting his gaze from Raymond to Tamara. "You know why I don't like rich patient?"

Tamara shook her head.

"Because they think they get to make the rules. You can't make me stay here, you can't do this, you can't do that, you can't, you can't and you can't."

Raymond rested his hands on the table as his lips curved into a small smile. "I can see you're prejudiced against my kind."

Dr. Morgan smirked. "Your kind? How quickly you forget your roots."

"You see that's what you should have thought of before you made your prejudiced statement. I had a humble beginning, and I haven't forgotten my roots."

"Guys!" Tamara yelled. "Stop this."

"C'mon, Tamara," Raymond said. "Doc and I are just joking here. Right, Doc?" he asked, smiling.

Dr. Morgan nodded and smiled back.

Tamara smiled. "If that's a joke, then you both have a weird sense of humor." Her countenance turned serious. "Ray, you should stay here. Take your treatment and get better."

He glanced at Tamara. "I can't. And you know why."

Tamara gave him a knowing look, and then glanced back at Dr. Morgan. Before she could say anything, he shook his head and said, "Don't even ask me, Tamara. Don't!"

"Please, Dr. Morgan," she pleaded.

"No, Tamara. How is it going to be? I'll go to him every day to inject him with Dimercaprol? No, it doesn't work that way. He has to stay here. I have to watch his improvement. I have to carry out a lot of tests to be sure that the med is not posing any risks."

A small sigh escaped from between her lips. She kept gazing at Dr. Morgan, her eyes pleading with him.

"Tamara!"

"You owe me, Dr. Morgan!"

"Don't play that card, Tamara." Dr. Morgan replied. "When you saved my marriage, I paid you for your work, didn't I?"

"But you said if I ever needed anything..."

"Tamara," he said in a conceding manner.

"Thanks, Dr. Morgan."

He cut her off. "Before you start thanking me, I have to report this to the appropriate authorities. There's no going back on that!"

"No, you can't. Please!" Raymond said.

"Why not? If your poisoning was as a result of some kind of environmental contamination, I need to let them know before other people get hurt!"

"I agree with him, Ray," Tamara said. "You should let him."

He looked at Tamara, his voice lower. "What if it's Dahlia, like you predicted?"

Before Tamara could give a response, Dr. Morgan interrupted. "Do you think this Dahlia is the one responsible for your arsenic poisoning?"

"No," Raymond replied. "Mara thinks so, but we're not sure. We have no proof yet."

Tamara interrupted. "But I'm trying very hard to prove that she is the one doing this."

Dr. Morgan was quiet for a long second. If Tamara hadn't known him for a long time, she would think the expression on his face was guilt. Tamara wondered what he was feeling guilty about.

"Alright, I'll hold off on reporting the case." He turned to Tamara. "But I give you just 48 hours to show me some kind of evidence that Dahlia is responsible for this. That way, I can rest assured that it's not some kind of environmental pollution and no one else is getting hurt."

"Okay," Tamara replied. "I promise I'll get you a proof before the end of today."

"Good," he replied. "And I'm willing to come to you every day to administer the Dimercaprol."

"Oh, no! That's too much to ask for," Raymond said. "You've done enough already. I'll come in every day to get my treatment."

"Okay," Dr. Morgan replied. Before he could go further, his pager beeped. He took a quick look at it, and then looked back at Tamara and Raymond. "Duty calls." He stood up from the chair, looking at Raymond. "Mr. Connor, you should get your first dose of Dimercaprol today. Go to the front desk. They'll check you in, take your medical info and prep you."

"Okay," Raymond replied.

Raymond and Tamara stood up from the chair.

"Thanks for everything, Doc," Raymond said.

"You're welcome," Dr. Morgan replied, extending a hand to Raymond. "Nice to meet you, Mr. Connor."

Raymond took his hand. "Call me Raymond, please."

Dr. Morgan smiled and gave Tamara a quick hug, hurrying out.

Tamara and Raymond walked out of the office. Hearing whispers and a few nurses gazing and pointing at Raymond, she felt the need to lean in a little closer. It might appear too petty of her, but she didn't care. Raymond's heart was crowded already, and there was no room for anyone else.

"What are you doing?" Raymond asked, leaning a bit closer and whispering in her ear.

She smiled back. "Claiming what's mine."

He shrugged. "At least we agree on something."

At that moment, they reached the front desk. And, of course, they had to go through a reception-ist who was already smitten by Raymond's good looks and his supposedly fat pocket. "May I have your ID, please?" she asked, giving a very bright smile that Tamara recognized to be more than just a smile.

"Sure," he replied, flashing her one of his panty-dropping smiles. And then he gently handed her his driver's license.

He was turning on the charm for fun and Tamara felt a stab of jealousy. Leaning back on the desk, her eyes went slowly to his. "And what is it that we agreed on?"

"That I'm yours, and you're mine." His voice was low.

Standing opposite her, he pressed himself against her. She felt him. Felt his body touch hers, and felt a tingling sensation between her legs. She shivered and reminded herself that they were still in public, telling herself to step away a little. But he had her cornered. So, she swallowed hard, trying to change the subject. "You're going to begin your treatment today?"

He nodded gently. "That's what the doc said," he said. Still leaning close to her, he pulled his brows together in a gentle frown. "But there's something weird about him, though."

"What?"

"I don't know. I can't just put my finger on it. His name sounds so familiar, and it feels as if I've seen his face before."

"Dr. Morgan is a good man. I trust him," she said. Reassuringly, she gently placed her hands on his chest. "You have nothing to worry about, okay?"

He nodded slowly as his eyes came boldly to meet hers. His gaze made her shiver. She suddenly felt the need to swallow. She did, and then her lips felt dry. She licked her lips, but if she were being honest with herself, she felt like kissing him instead. Right there. Right now. But she couldn't. She wouldn't. She had told him they needed a break from their relationship. And Ray hadn't decided if he wanted to go public with their relationship yet — and this was definitely a public place. But if he didn't want to go public with the relationship, why was he leaning inappropriately close to her in public.

"I have to go," she said.

"I'll walk you to the car," he said. The receptionist returned his ID. "I'll be right back," he said to the receptionist.

They walked to her car. Tamara rested her back on the car and before she realized what was going on, Ray leaned even closer. So close he could feel his breath on her face. For one second, she thought he might kiss her. She was aware that she should be moving away right about now, but she couldn't. Instead, she closed her eyes gently, expecting to feel a small kiss on her lips or on her cheek. But then, he leaned closer and whispered, "Have a nice day," in his low, deep voice.

Tamara's eyes opened to catch a devilish grin spread across his face. Her hands became a fist and hit his chest playfully. "What was that?"

He drew back slightly, sliding his hands into his pockets and shrugging. "What? I thought you said we're taking a short break. We shouldn't be kissing, should we?"

"Whatever!" she said. Opening her car door, she threw her purse on the passenger's seat and turned back at Raymond. "I've got to run. I have to prove to you and Dr. Morgan that Dahlia is responsible for this problem. My clock is ticking."

"Okay. Be careful, please." He opened his arms to give her a goodbye hug.

She drew back slightly, shaking her head gently and smiling. "No hugs."

"What?!"

She nodded. "Payback."

"Mara!"

FOUR

Tamara had a headache. It started right after she drove off the parking lot at the hospital. Raymond was intimate with her in public. Maybe not that intimate, but he leaned very close and almost kissed her. That was supposed to be a good thing, right? But why did he insist on keeping things low in the relationship? And why the hell was he insisting on keeping her as his mistress? Just a few weeks ago, he was hell-bent on divorcing Dahlia. So why was he finding it difficult to do that now?

Oh! And so much for taking a break from their relationship! When he almost kissed her, she just stood there, mooning over him like a teenage girl expecting a kiss on her first date. She should have pushed him away, but with Ray, she just couldn't be that strong.

Maybe she was pushing him too hard. Maybe asking him to choose her was too much. Her head ached even more, so she told herself to stop thinking about Raymond for the moment.

She parked her car in the parking lot at her office building and strode into the conference room. Her heart skipped more than a beat when she saw

Drake. She had spoken to him on phone that morning, but seeing him now was totally different. He looked hurt.

"Hello, Tamara," Drake said.

And he definitely wasn't his usual self. Drake would never be this gentle and calm and formal with her. He would have teased her, flirted with her and tried to make her laugh. But now, he was just calm. Still handsome, but calm. And Tamara could swear she saw circles beneath his eyes. He hadn't slept well because of her. Or maybe that was what she wanted to believe.

"Hey, Tamara," Megan said.

"Hi, good morning," Tamara replied, trying to pull herself together. She looked toward Drake, but avoided making eye contact. "Did you find anything on Rachel Brock?"

"Yeah, I did." He reached for a folder and handed it to Tamara.

Dropping her purse on the table, she took the folder from him. His hands touched hers, and for the first time ever, his touch caused vibrations in her. She shuddered, and the folder slipped off her hands. As soon as she squatted to pick up the folder, Drake bent to pick up the folder and then their gaze met. She was frozen. For the first time in a long time, she saw deep into his heart. In his eyes, she saw something. Loneliness. And she felt guilty that she couldn't be the woman for him, the woman he needed.

"What is wrong with both of you?' Megan asked.

Tamara broke the gaze, rose to her feet and cleared her throat. "Nothing. Why?"

Megan shrugged. "Well, you two are acting weird. You're being too formal with each other. Like there's tension between you."

Tamara gave a sarcastic smile. "Really?" She didn't wait for a response. Trying desperately to change the subject, she looked at Drake and asked, "What did you find out about Rachel Brock?"

"Rachel Brock was one of the numerous domestic staff of the Connors. After she had Raymond, she kept the secret about who the father was and continued working with the Connors. Not long after that, James Connor was terribly ill, and it was discovered that his meal had been poisoned. James Connor received treatment and was healthy again. But Rachel Brock was charged with attempted murder. She confessed to the crime and was sentenced to life imprisonment with possibility of parole. Raymond must have hated his mother for this. Never visited her in prison. You can't blame him, though. He went from one foster home to another after being abandoned by both his parents."

Tamara swallowed hard. Now she understood what Raymond meant about history not repeating itself. If she was right, if Dahlia was responsible for contaminating Raymond's food with arsenic, then she would end up like Rachel. And then their son would grow up without a mother, and possibly without a father, too, if the poisoning could not be treated. Tamara's heart tightened in pain.

She understood him perfectly now. The reason he didn't want to get the police involved, and the reason he so much didn't want to believe that Dahlia could be responsible for everything. Most of all, she understood the reason he never talked about his mother. Her heart went out to Raymond. How lonely his childhood must have been!

Opening the folder Drake gave her, she read through the documents. When she turned to the next page, she saw a newspaper clipping. As she read through, she saw the article titled *Rachel Brock Sentenced to Life in Prison*. The woman in the photograph shared a striking resemblance to Raymond. Staring at the picture for a long moment, she at last looked at Megan and Drake.

"She didn't do it!" Tamara said.

"What do you mean she didn't do it?" Megan asked.

"She confessed to the crime!" Drake said.

"I know," Tamara replied, "but something tells me she didn't do it."

Before they could respond, they heard footsteps behind them. Tamara closed the folder and turned to see who it was.

"Sherry!" Tamara said as she set eyes on her. "What are you doing here? I fired you!"

"I know. But you said I'm fired until Drake can confirm if I was telling the truth."

Drake interrupted. "She was telling the truth," Drake said, looking at Tamara. "She cheated to get into Law School and Dahlia tried to use that against her. Dahlia blackmailed her into betraying you."

Tamara lifted a shoulder in a shrug. "Still, you're fired."

"Please, Tamara," Sherry pleaded. "I would never deliberately betray you."

"But you betrayed me!"

"Tamara, please."

Tamara picked her purse from the table. "No, Sherry. I need people I can trust around me. I have so much going on that I don't have time to bother about one untrustworthy employee." She finished and began to walk out of the conference room. Before she got to the door, she heard Drake's voice.

"Tamara! Please, give her one more chance. I believe she has learned her lesson and wouldn't make the same mistake again," Drake pleaded.

She held Drake in high esteem and respected him so much that she couldn't refuse him a favor. "Drake, please do not ask me to take Sherry back. I don't want to refuse you, and I don't want to take her back."

"Tamara, please," he pleaded.

"Why are you pleading on her behalf?" she asked, her voice louder and harsher than she had intended it to be.

"Because this is not you," he replied. "You always give people second chances. You forgive easily. And Sherry was naïve and scared and made a mistake. Just forgive her this one time."

She considered it for a while, and then she shook her head. "No," she said and turned to open the door.

"You need me!"

Sherry's voice brought her to a halt. "What?"

"You need me, Tamara," Sherry said again. "You're good at your job. You save marriages, and you always try to do the right thing, but you never know when you're crossing the line. I'm here to help us all not to cross the line. I'm the one who reminds you that it is wrong to intrude on our client's privacy. I'm the only who can disagree with you when you're going too far. I'm the good side of you that you don't want to lose. You need me!"

Tamara walked back to where Sherry stood and glared at her. "Nice speech, but you're still fired." She turned to Drake. "You. My office. Now!"

****

She should have seen it coming.

She should have suspected something wasn't right when Drake hired that girl. Ray was right — she should widen her suspicions. But she trusted Drake. She had known him since high school, and he had never given her any reason to doubt him. Till now!

Walking into her office, she threw her purse on the table and waited for Drake to walk in. As soon as Drake walked in and shut the door, she folded her arms across her chest and looked at him. This time, she was not afraid to look him straight in the eyes.

"Why were you pleading on her behalf?" she asked.

"Because I pitied her. You used to be like that girl, Tamara. You remember when we used to work at Keller & Associates? You made several mistakes, and you were trying so hard to make an impression. You were once like Sherry."

She narrowed her gaze, as if looking deep into his soul to get answers. "Are you sure that's the only reason you pleaded on her behalf?"

"Yes. She reminds me of you when you started."

Tamara unfolded her arms and withdrew her gaze, trying not to make him realize she was suspicious of him. "Tell me, Drake, why did you hire Sherry in the first place?"

"Because she was the best of all the people I interviewed for the position."

Tamara began to pace in circles around Drake. "And before the interview, you had never met Sherry before, correct?"

He nodded slowly. "Correct."

"And all the time she worked here, you two never worked on a special case/project together?"

"No. I don't understand what you mean by special case."

Before she could respond, he gave her a suspicious look. "Are you interrogating me?"

She stopped pacing and stood opposite him, only a few strides apart. "You tell me. Because right now, I don't know what to think."

"Maybe you can give more of an explanation. I don't quite understand." His voice was shaky, and a hint of anger was spreading across his face.

"You hired Sherry! And then it turned out Sherry was working for Dahlia. I fired her, but you want me to hire her again, despite the fact that she betrayed this law firm. And recently you said you've always been in love with me and…"

He cut her off. "So you think because I'm in love with you, that I am psychopathic enough to want

Raymond dead. You think I'm involved in the conspiracy to kill Raymond. You think I'm working
with Dahlia."

She studied his face a moment. "Because that
would be so untrue?"

He scowled, Tamara's accusing eyes stabbing
him worse than a sword to his heart. "You've
known me longer than most. You think I'm capable
of such a thing?!" he growled.

Tamara saw the anger and sincerity in his eyes,
and she regretted ever doubting him. What was she
thinking? It's Drake. Drake would never hurt a fly.
Walking closer to him, she tried to hold his hands.
"Drake," she called her voice gentle.

Drake's fist tightened. "Don't touch me!"

"I'm sorry for being paranoid. I just don't know
who to trust anymore."

"Tamara, I've been with you since childhood.
I've been with you through tough times and terrible
times. We've been through too much together. Just
you and I. I've shared your pain and your tears,
even though you never paid attention to mine."

"I'm sorry…"

"I thought we were friends. I thought we could
trust each other no matter what."

"Drake! Please…"

"What's the point of working together if you
can't trust me?"

"Drake," she said, holding his hand gently. "I'm
sorry."

He jerked his hand from her hold. "You know
what, Tamara? I QUIT!!!" he said and reached for
the door.

Tamara followed. "Drake, wait!"

"I'm done living my life for you. I'm done putting my life on hold for you. I'm done waiting for you!"

Opening the door, he hurried out.

Tamara ran after him. "Drake, please wait. Drake! Let's talk about this."

In the lobby, Megan saw her running after Drake. She walked closer to her. "Tamara, what's the problem?"

She halted and watched Drake leave the building. Tears gathered in Tamara's eyes, and she hated herself so much for ruining a precious friendship. "Drake just quit," she replied.

"What? Why?" Megan asked.

Tamara swallowed the lump in her throat. "It's just you and me now."

As Tamara stood there, all she could do was think that Dahlia was the cause of this. It's because of her that her friendship with Drake got ruined. It's because of her that she couldn't even enjoy a relationship with the man she loved. Enough is enough!

She took her cellphone and made a quick call to Dahlia. It was high time someone put a stop to all her games.

FIVE

Tamara Price had always considered herself to be a very smart, canny and intelligent woman. Yet with all her intelligence, she wasn't able to protect Raymond from being poisoned. She wasn't even able to convince Raymond that his wife, Dahlia, was responsible for contaminating his food with tiny bits of arsenic and intended to keep doing it until it killed him.

Now she had no choice but to play her last card.

It was an unpleasant task, but Tamara needed to do it tonight.

Sitting in her car at the parking lot of Mosaic nightclub, Tamara gazed out through the night-darkened window, her eyes searching for any sign of Dahlia.

The thought of what she was about to do sickened her, and she felt an irritation in her stomach. Trying to control the itch to throw up, she held her breath and consoled herself with the thought that she was doing it for Raymond.

A car parked opposite her and from the license plate, she could tell it was Dahlia.

Gently, Tamara took her cellphone, got out of the car and walked toward Dahlia's car. Cautiously, she opened the passenger's door and got in, placing her cellphone on the center console of the car as she sat.

"You wanted to talk?" Dahlia said, her steely, cold eyes gazing at her.

"Yes," Tamara replied.

"What is it? I've only got a little time to spare."

Tamara's blood boiled. Her fist clenched and her eyes flashed with fire. She wanted to say, *you know what, screw you!* But then she calmed down, reminding herself that she was doing this for Raymond.

"You win. I lose," Tamara said quietly. The words took a long moment to come out of her mouth, but when they did, she wished she could take them all back. She had never accepted defeat before, especially to her archenemy. But there was always a first time for everything.

Putting her hand to her ear, Dahlia leaned closer. "What did you say?"

Tamara sucked in her breath. "You win. I lose," she repeated.

Dahlia gave a loud laugh without humor, beating the steering wheel as she did. "And it took you this long to know that I always win. How did you realize it?"

"You threatened to destroy the two things I loved most—Raymond and my job. My career almost got destroyed when you broke that news, and now Raymond has tested positive for arsenic poisoning. You did it, I'm sure."

"Of course I did it." She looked over and gave another of her dry laughs. *"If you so much as hurt Raymond or even pull a strand of hair from his body, I will track you down. I will hunt you, and I will rain down a godly lake that burns with fire and brimstone upon you,"* she said, mimicking the way Tamara said it. "You remember when you threatened me like that?"

Tamara shut her eyes and forced out a tear. "I'm sorry, Dahlia. I am truly sorry."

"WOW! I feel on top of the world right now," Dahlia said. "The strong, powerful Tamara Price accepting defeat. I'm definitely on top of the world."

"Dahlia, please spare Raymond's life. I promise I'll handle your divorce well. I'll make sure you get half, if not all, of the Connor wealth. But Raymond doesn't have to die. Please…"

"Tamara, I wish it was that simple," Dahlia said, her countenance suddenly soft as if Tamara had started a sensitive conversation. She looked at Tamara and blinked. "You see, our one-year wedding anniversary party is in a few days. Raymond will be dead on or before that day."

Tamara didn't have to force the tears out. It came freely. Placing her hand over Dahlia's, she looked into her eyes and pleaded. "Dahlia, please. Please spare Raymond's life. Not for my sake, but for your son's sake. You said you don't want him to grow up without a father, right? For your son's sake, please spare his life. If it pleases you, I'll stay away from him. Raymond will be for you and your son alone. Even if we are not together, I'm happy as long as he is alive somewhere."

Dahlia looked thoughtful, almost sad. "You love him very much, don't you?"

Tamara nodded gently.

Dahlia smiled sadly. "I love him, too," she said. And then her smile disappeared. "But this is beyond me. It's more than me." Her voice became very shaky. "Everything has been planned. It's not in my hands to decide if Raymond lives or dies. I don't want him dead either." She blinked back tears. "Let's just keep praying that maybe by some miracle, he lives."

"Dahlia, please," Tamara pleaded.

Too close to tears to speak further, Dahlia swallowed the lumps in her throat. "Goodnight, Tamara. And please, pray well."

Tamara took her phone and left Dahlia's car. When she got back to her car, she found the voice recorder on her phone and hit the play button.

You threatened to destroy the two things I loved most — Raymond and my job. My career almost got destroyed when you broke that news, and now Raymond has tested positive for arsenic poisoning. You did it, I'm sure."

"Of course I did it."

She pressed the stop button and smiled to herself. Task completed. Dahlia had a lot to answer for.

****

Tamara Price smelled trouble and danger all around her. Dahlia said Raymond would be dead on or before their wedding anniversary party. That was exactly what danger smelled like. She had to get to the bottom of this. She had to make sure the plan to kill Raymond didn't happen. *You have to be strong,* was all her brain kept telling her. And the first step to that was to warn Raymond.

She picked up her cellphone, but before she could dial Raymond's number, the phone rang. She stared at the phone for some seconds, but didn't recognize the number. She thought it might be a worried client, so she pressed the green button.

"Tamara Price, how may I help you?"

"This call is from the city police department. Your friend Drake Johnson is being held for drunk driving. He requested to talk to you…"

Tamara wasn't sure she paid attention to the rest of the conversation. She got in her car and drove speedily to the police department. As she drove, she kept wondering what was wrong with Drake. He was many things—a flirt, a womanizer, a jerk, but not a drunkard. Even if he had a little too much drink, he knew better than to drive under the influence of alcohol.

When she got to the police department, she posted his bail and arranged to get him out. After about an hour, when Drake was finally released, she noticed that he had sobered up a bit.

Without uttering a word, they walked slowly to Tamara's car. She went for the driver's seat as Drake eased himself into the passenger's seat. For one long second, Tamara didn't start the engine. She considered if she should say something or just let him be, but the part of her that worried about him told her to speak.

"Driving under the influence! What did you think you were doing?"

He frowned. "Don't talk to me as if you're responsible for me! You're not my mother!" he said, his voice hardened.

"I am your friend…"

"That doesn't give you the right to be responsible for me."

The edge to her own voice surprised her. "You gave me the right to be responsible for you when you chose to call me to get your ass out of custody!"

Drake gritted his teeth and leaned closer. "So this is about the fact that I called you to come get me out. I'm sorry." His voice didn't sound apologetic. "I won't call out to you next time."

"Oh! So you think I'm angry because you called me for help?" Tamara was getting angry now. "I'm angry because I'm worried about you. In all the years I've known you, I've never seen you drunk let alone stain your record by driving under the influence. Look, I know you're hurting, and you're running away from me, and you won't let me help you…"

"Help me?" he said, a sarcastic smile spreading lightly across his face before quickly disappearing. "Help me," he said again. "You can't be the sickness and the cure at the same time."

"What do you mean?"

"For years I've stayed by your side. I watched your back. I protected you. I waited for you. I dried your tears. I gave you a shoulder to cry on every time you needed one. I helped mend your heart every time it was broken. I didn't have a life of my own because I was waiting for you. I'm always there for you! My whole life is controlled by what you want and what you need—and doing everything that makes you happy. And it's okay that you said you're not in love with me. I can live with that. But you looking into my eyes and accusing me of being involved in the conspiracy to kill your boyfriend was too much. It was more than I could take. It means after all this time, you don't trust me. At all. And it hurts to know I'm dispensable to you, and I've wasted all those years staying by your side!" He paused for a second, as if thinking about what to say. "You can't help me. You're the reason I'm like this." He struggled to make the words come out as he lowered his face. "You're the one destroying me, so you can't help me."

She sat there, watching him in silence, and then her stare turned into a deadly glare. "You're destroying yourself. I'm not the one destroying you. You chose to destroy yourself. I didn't ask you to stay by my side, and I didn't ask you to live your life for me, but you did anyway. It was your choice, not mine! You waited for me because, in your mind, the friendship we had meant more than friendship. But it doesn't. It's just friendship! Nothing more, nothing less." She swallowed. She knew she was being too hard, and it was hurting her. too, but it was the right thing to do to wake him up from his fairytale, to stop him from holding on to her and destroying himself. "Don't get me wrong—I appreciate all you've done for me. I appreciate you so much, and you're wrong to think that you are dispensable, because, really, you're indispensable to me. But that doesn't mean I want you to keep waiting for me. I rejected you, I accused you falsely, and

I am so sorry for that. But you don't get to drink your life away because of that. So snap out of your self-pity and self-destruction mode! It is not who you are! Snap out of it now!"

For several seconds, no one said anything. Tamara was waiting for him to respond, to say something, but he didn't. Silence suffocated the both of them. Finally, Drake raised his face and looked gently at Tamara. "I'll take a cab," he said. His voice was low, slightly above a whisper.

"Drake!"

Before she could say more, he opened the passenger's door and stepped out of the car.

"Drake! Drake!"

When he didn't respond, she stopped calling him and watched as he got into a taxi and the driver sped away. She stared out into nothingness for a while, and then rested her head on the steering wheel in frustration.

SIX

You're an idiot! You're an idiot!

Tamara murmured under her breath as she drove home. Why on earth did she say all those mean words? Why did she tell the man who was by her side all these years that he was destroying himself by waiting for her? *Why did you say that? You idiot,* she said through clenched teeth, and then hit the steering wheel with the heel of her hand.

But it was the truth. The truth had to be told even if it hurt. Drake needed to be put back on the right track, and that was what she did. She need not blame herself for it.

But no matter how much she tried to console herself, she still felt bad for hurting him, for being responsible for all the pain and anger consuming him.

Gently, she drove into her garage and forced herself to walk out. Noticing a black Bentley parked in front of her house, she knew Raymond was around. She peered through the car window to check if Raymond was there waiting for her, but the windows were tinted and she couldn't see anything. She was about to tap the window lightly when her eyes caught the tiny reflection of lights coming from her house. She guessed they were coming from her HDTV. Raymond was in her house! *How the hell did he get in?* She asked herself as she walked to the house and opened the front door.

Raymond turned down the volume on the TV and glanced at the door. "Hey," he said in greeting.

"Hey. How did you get in?"

"I let myself in," he replied. "I still have your spare key. Remember?"

Tamara threw her purse on the couch as her eyes gave a quick assessment of Raymond. The sleeves of his t-shirt fit too tight over his muscular arms, exposing the outline of the hard muscles of his arms and shoulders. She imagined how it always felt to slide her hands down his arm and... She swallowed hard and told her sex drive to shut up. "What part of we need to take a break from this relationship do you not understand?"

He relaxed his back on the couch. "Taking a break was your idea, and I didn't agree to it."

She stood there and didn't respond.

"Why are you in a bad mood?" he asked.

She still didn't respond.

"Come here," he said softly but firmly, and patted the couch next to him. "Come here and tell daddy who peed on your birthday cake?"

She managed a weak smile as she walked very slowly to sit beside him on the couch. "I have too much going on around me. My life is disorganized. Everything is falling apart..."

Wrapping his hand around her waist, he pulled her closer. "Nothing is falling apart, baby. Now why would you say that?"

She rested her head peacefully on his strong chest. "I acted like an idiot today."

He slowly caressed her hair. "Mara, your idiocy is still smarter than some people's wisdom."

"I don't think so."

"Well, I think so. Tell me what happened."

"I'm in love with a man who is partially in love with me and would rather throw a large wedding anniversary party for his wife instead of choosing to be with me. And I just found out that this man has a death sentence on his head. And if that were not enough, I pushed my friend away, accused him of being involved in the conspiracy to kill my dying boyfriend, and in an attempt to make things right, I said terrible things to him and made matters worse."

"First, you're a good person, and I believe whatever you said to Drake was something that had to be said. Drake is a man. And a man's ego is very strong. He needs to figure some things out for himself, so give him little time. He'll come around." Raymond paused for a moment and began to caress her hair. "And, second, you know there is only one woman I love—you."

She raised her face to look at him. "Really?"

Raymond nodded. "Yes, really," he replied, not taking his eyes away from her for a second. Ever so slowly and gently, Raymond held her face in his hands and pressed his lips against hers. The kiss started a fire within her, and she wanted more.

Raymond slowly broke off the kiss. Still holding her face in his hands, he stared back at her.

He kissed her again. It grew deeper. Wrapping his arms tightly around her, he drew her close against him. She ran her hands over his back as they kissed. His back was strong and warm. Loving the feel of his skin, she let her hands caress his chest and then his shoulders. Fire burnt through her veins as his lips moved briefly to her neck and then found her mouth again. In a long time, nothing had ever felt as good as Raymond kissing her like that. She felt herself melting into him everywhere their body touched. When she finally broke the kiss and pulled apart slightly, both their hearts were pounding.

Tamara cleared her throat, gazing into his strong brown eyes. "Ray, you, um... you know that I don't want to..."

"I know," he broke in softly. "You want us to take a break. You want to be more than a mistress, more than a sex object. I know." He reached for her hand and placed soft tiny kisses on her palm to her wrist. "Mara, it's OK. We'll do whatever you want. I just want to be with you; I don't care."

Tamara nodded, lifted up her face and kissed him, so gently at first. Then she pressed closely against him as the kiss deepened, wrapping her hands around his neck as she lost herself to pure sensation.

Raymond broke the kiss very gently. "So what do you mean by there's a death sentence on my head?"

Tamara pulled away and reached for her purse. Searching for her phone, she glanced at Raymond. "You won't like what you're about to hear."

"Tell me anyway."

By that time, she had found the voice recorder on her phone. Looking at Raymond, she asked, "Are you sure?"

"Yes."

Tamara hit the play button.

"You threatened to destroy the two things I loved most — Raymond and my job. My career almost got destroyed when you broke that news, and now Raymond tested positive for arsenic poisoning. You did it, I'm sure."

"Of course I did it."

"Everything has been planned. It's not in my hands to decide if Raymond lives or dies. I don't want him dead either... Let's just keep praying so that maybe by some miracle, he lives."

Raymond let out a deep breath and sank his back on the couch. He wiped the sweat from his forehead, and then held his face in his palms for several minutes.

Tamara could see the rise and fall of his chest. When Raymond was breathing hard like this, holding his hands in his face and sweating on his forehead like that, it was a sign that he was disturbed. Hurt. Angry.

"Maybe you should cancel the wedding anniversary party for now..."

"No," he broke in. "I can't. The wedding anniversary party is just a cover story. You remember when the story broke that you and I were having an affair and the news almost ruined your law firm?"

Tamara nodded.

"Then you should remember that I released a story that I'm not having an affair with you. You were helping Dahlia and I fix our marriage and you did it perfectly. The wedding anniversary party is the evidence. Just to make the story, you know, believable. The party is to help save your law firm from scandal, and I'm not cancelling it. I should be able to do that much for you,"

Tamara sat closer, wrapping her arms around him. "You don't have to do anything for me."

"I wanted so much for this not to be true," he said, almost as if talking to himself.

"You mean Dahlia?" Tamara asked.

"Yes. I prayed. I hoped. I wanted her not to be the one trying to kill me. I wanted it not to be her. It should have been an angry client or one of those selfish directors at Connor Corp. Anyone. Just not Dahlia."

Tamara caressed his chest and modulated her voice to soothe him. "Don't blame Dahlia too much. After speaking with her, I stopped blaming her, too. It seems like she's just a puppet in a conspiracy to kill you…"

When she said the word "kill", Tamara felt his chest rising and falling beneath her palm, his heart beating faster than before. She felt the need to reassure him. "Ray, you're not going to die, okay? We are a step higher than them. We discovered the poisoning before it was too late and you're taking the treatment."

Raymond shoved her hands off him and stood up sternly. "I have to go."

In a split second, Tamara was on her feet. "Go where?"

He reached for his car keys, and then turned back to look at her, his eyes flashing pure anger. "To talk to her! I need answers."

Hands on her waist, Tamara stood firmly. "You aren't going anywhere!"

"Mara, I've done enough for her. I tried to trust her, protect her and believed that she was not capable of murder. I have done more than a husband should. I've endured too much! Enough is enough! Get out of my way!"

"What in the name of everything reasonable do you think you're doing?" she asked, her tone hardened.

"Putting an end to this!"

There was a kind of wildness in his eyes that betrayed an angry spirit. Tamara knew he was consumed with anger. It wasn't easy learning that his wife, the mother of his son, had been trying to kill him. She understood his anger, but wouldn't let the anger lead him into making a mistake. "This is not the best way to handle this!"

Raymond scowled. "This is the only way I know. If you know any other way, let me hear it." He swept Tamara aside and began to walk away. "But until then, you need to get out of my way!"

Tamara ran to catch up with him, threw herself in front of him and then rested her back on the door to prevent him from getting to it. "Don't do this! Don't ruin everything!"

Raymond shot her a glare. "Don't try to stop me, Mara!"

"If Dahlia finds out—if the people behind this find out— that you know about the arsenic poisoning, they will find another way to kill you!"

"Dahlia knows that you know. She knows you're going to tell me!"

Tamara held him by the arm and looked straight into his eyes. "Trust me, I have a plan. I'll handle it."

Raymond jerked his arm away from Tamara's hold, pushing her away from the door as he did. "Don't try to stop me!"

"Ray! Ray! Trust me. I have a plan. I can handle this!"

Ignoring her, he opened the door and walked out.

SEVEN

Raymond slammed his foot on the brake and parked his car in his expensive garage, his heart almost exploding with anger. He hardly had the patience to lock the car when he rushed toward the front door of his house and pushed it open.

"Dahlia!" he roared, his voice thundering through the house.

"Honey," Dahlia replied. Very slowly, she sat up on the couch, her face wrinkled as she stretched out her arms. "I was sitting on the couch waiting for you to come back home." She used her palm to cover her mouth as she yawned. "I must have dozed off."

Walking speedily closer to Dahlia, he yelled, "You need to start talking now!"

"About what?"

"Why you're so evil! Why you're hell-bent on frustrating my life! Who sent you into my life?"

She pulled her brows together in confusion. "What? What are you talking about?"

Every look of pretend innocence she gave him made his heart grow more furious. He walked closer to her. Before he could say any further, Tamara's voice kept repeating itself in his mind. *Don't do this. Don't ruin everything.*

Trying to forget Tamara's warning, he walked closer to Dahlia, face close and eyes locked together. "I can have the police right here in the next few seconds and let them arrest you..."

Raymond could see the fear in her eyes, but she covered it up well as she crouched to pick up the baby from the couch. "Your voice is loud and harsh. He's going to wake up."

"Leave my son out of this! He is sleeping."

In a split second, the baby began to cry. Raymond could swear he saw her pinch the baby's arm. "You hurt your child just to stop my anger? What type of a mother are you?"

"The type that cares about her child and her husband." She concentrated on the baby. "His diaper must be wet. Or maybe he's hungry."

His fatherly senses kicked in. He couldn't stand watching his son cry. "Give him to me. I'll change his diaper. You get his food."

She gave the baby to him. "Thanks."

"Don't thank me. He's my son! Is he not?"

She nodded briefly and ran off to the kitchen to get the baby's food.

Raymond picked up the wipes and the diaper. As he sat changing the baby's diaper, he noticed the diaper wasn't wet. It was probably just recently changed. At that moment, he understood Dahlia perfectly well. The woman had intentionally pinched her child's arm just to suppress her husband's rage. Dahlia was devious and cunning, and Tamara had been right about her along.

The baby stopped crying, but Dahlia hadn't returned with his food yet. Holding the baby very gently in his arms, he walked toward the kitchen to find Dahlia. A whispering voice caught his attention as he moved closer to the kitchen. He halted and listened in.

I think he knows… I'm not sure. I think he knows…

At that moment, Dahlia raised her face and caught him standing there. Very quickly, she dropped the call and said, "I was… um… talking to my brother."

"You're fine," he replied, grabbing the baby's bottle from her. "I came for his food."

She took the bottle back from him. "Let me feed him."

Raymond nodded, and then held the baby close enough for her to put the bottle in his mouth. As the baby began to suck, Dahlia squeezed the bottle with a firm steady pressure.

After a few seconds, he stopped sucking.

"I don't think he's hungry," he said as he looked at Dahlia. Their faces were so close together that their noses almost touched. Raymond quickly broke the gaze by glancing at the baby. "He looks like he wants to sleep."

"Yeah,' she replied and reached for the baby. "Let me take him to bed."

"I'll take him," Raymond said.

Raymond led the way to the baby's room. As he laid him gently on the bed, Dahlia sat close, watching keenly as Raymond helped their baby to bed. When Raymond was sure that his son was deep asleep, he gently caressed his hair and placed a tiny soft kiss on his forehead. "Daddy loves you very much," he whispered.

Cautiously, Dahlia leaned closer and placed a soft kiss on the baby's cheek. And then she sat down on the couch next to the bed. "You wanted to say something to me," she said, glancing at Raymond.

He nodded. "Yeah." His voice was only slightly above a whisper to avoid waking the baby. "I said I could have the police here right now and have them arrest you for being sexually involved with a minor," he lied. "I want you out of my life so bad that I'd threaten to do that, exposing the secret I helped bury." He paused for a second and sat on the couch next to her. "But right now, you and I are taking care of Richard together, and it reminds me how much my family means to me. I want every day to be like this, Dahlia. Show love to each other and share part of the love with our son, Richard. I want the rest of our days to be like this."

Surprise was evident on her face, and her voice caught for an instant. When she finally found her voice, she replied, "Me, too. And thank you for coming home today. It means a lot to Richard and me."

He nodded.

Carefully, Dahlia sat closer. "We can start over, right? A new beginning. You'll forgive everything I did wrong. The ones you know and the ones you don't know about."

He held her hand in his. "I'm willing to try."

She nodded. Her lips curved into a smile as she gazed passionately into his eyes.

Raymond didn't take his eyes off her. He kept staring. Even in the near darkness, her big brown eyes fascinated him. Faces close together, Raymond leaned in as his lips touched hers.

Her full lips received his in a warm kiss. As their tongue twined together, it felt like two lost souls reconnecting again.

He broke the kiss and watched her open her eyes. When she did, her eyes were naked with emotion. She wanted him, he knew that. But still…

"Will you ever be able to love me like you loved Tamara?" she asked.

Raymond lowered his face gently, contemplating on whether to tell her the harsh truth. A few seconds later, he lifted up his face and looked at her. "I want to be honest with you, Dahlia. I can try to love you. I can love you. I know I can. But what I felt for Mara, it's different. I love Mara from my soul. And one only gets to feel that once in a lifetime."

"And you can't choose to love me that way?"

"Dahlia, we don't choose who to love or who not to love. Love just claims our heart as it wills."

Disappointment spread across her face, and Raymond saw it. He squeezed her hand and leaned closer to her, watching her eyes to make sure she saw the assurance in his eyes. "Hey, honey, I'm not with Mara now. Not anymore. I'm with you. We're going to be okay, I promise. We will be alright. We will make us work."

She nodded and smiled.

Raymond kissed her again.

She tilted her head to make the kiss even deeper. Holding tightly to him, her hands went under his t-shirt and caressed his stomach, then slowly up his chest and arms. Her touch was enough to cause a stir in his manhood, but he had it all under control.

He pulled away very gently.

Eyes still slightly closed, Dahlia couldn't take her hands off him. "You want us to go to bed together?"

Placing a soft kiss on her cheeks, he replied, "No, let's take things slow this time," he said gently but firmly. "I want things to be different this time."

She nodded.

"I'll take you to your room."

Lifting her up, he carried her to her room. When he placed her on the bed, he leaned in and kissed her. "Goodnight," he whispered.

He could hardly wait to get back to his room before placing a call to Tamara. As soon as he made sure he was alone, he dialed Tamara's number.

He sat calmly on the bed. "Hey," he said. Almost immediately he heard her breath on the phone.

"Hey," she replied.

"I'm sorry. I shouldn't have yelled and walked out like that."

"You're fine. I understand how you must have felt." She paused for a few seconds and then asked, "How is your treatment going with Dr. Morgan?"

"Good. I feel as if I'm getting better already."

For the next few seconds, no one said anything. The silence roared in his ears.

Finally, he decided to speak. "I didn't do it. I didn't confront her like I said I would."

"What stopped you?"

"I wanted to. I almost did. But then I overheard her phone conversation. I figured out that you were right. Confronting her will only make them find other means to kill me. It won't let me find out who's behind this whole thing. So I put up an act as if I know nothing, as if I really want to make our marriage work. She played along, but I don't think she believes me."

"Dahlia is a smart woman. In time, she will figure it out. But keep up the act to buy us more time. First thing tomorrow morning, I'll start working on my plan."

He let out a deep breath. "Over and over again, you've proved that I need you more than you need me."

"We need each other, Ray. I am nothing without you. It's because of you that I am what I am. You've done too much for me, and this is my turn to do something for you."

"Still…"

She cut him off. "Let me help you, Ray," she pleaded. "I can help you if you let me."

He considered for a moment. "Okay."

"Good, but you have to tell me the whole truth. Don't hide anything. Don't try to protect Dahlia. You've protected her enough. So, please, tell me everything from the very beginning."

"The beginning," he said and relaxed his back on the bed. "Like I once told you, I met Dahlia again in Paris. Seems like she was aware that I'd be there, and she followed me. She told me the thing we did had become a baby. I remembered being angry at first. I remembered telling myself that I wanted my child raised in a home where his dad and mom lived happily together, something I never had the privilege to experience."

"Yeah, I know. And what you said about history not repeating itself... I found out about what happened with your mom."

Raymond didn't give a response. Mara started a discussion that he hated to talk about. Even though it happened more than twenty years ago, it still felt as if it were yesterday. It hurt that his dad didn't acknowledge him as his son until the late hour. It hurt that his mom took the law into her own hands and tried to kill his dad. He hated her for that. But the thing that hurt most was that he had to grow up and struggle alone without the help or comfort of his parents.

"It's ironic, is it not? The thing that men don't talk about is actually the thing that hurts them most," she said.

"Yeah," he replied. Desperately trying to change the subject, he continued, "So, I remember telling myself that the only way to prevent my son from having my kind of childhood was to marry his mother."

"And you got married to Dahlia," she finished for him.

"Yeah."

"But think back to the wedding. Is there anything else that happened? You know, a little detail that you might have left out?"

He tried to think back to one year ago. "Nothing. I've told you everything."

"Okay. What happened after the wedding?"

"I was ashamed of myself. I couldn't bring myself to look at you…"

She cut him off. "Skip that part."

"Mara!" he grimaced. "Not a day goes by that I don't regret that decision."

"I know. I'm not angry about it anymore."

"Thank you. So after the wedding, I suspected Dahlia of many things. I told my brother, Joe, about my suspicions. Joe told me that…" he suddenly stopped and decided against mentioning that. "We hired a private investigator to investigate Dahlia. The p.i. found nothing, so I stopped being suspicious of her."

"You stopped being suspicious? These past days I've been trying to warn you about someone trying to kill you, and you always tell me to stay out of it as if you know who is plotting against you."

"I thought I knew. You know, when you command as much wealth as I do, a lot of people want you dead. I wouldn't be surprised if it was one of the directors that was trying to kill me. But, Dahlia? I wasn't expecting it…"

"Dahlia and some powerful people," she corrected. "And you might be right. One of your directors might have hired Dahlia and placed her in your life to do the work."

"Still, Mara, if some of the directors at Connor Corp are involved in this, then it's dangerous for you to get involved."

"Ray!"

"You really don't understand, Mara. The people that I work with, they are rich, powerful and ruthless. They've funded a lot of political campaign and have a lot of politicians, police officials wrapped around their tiny fingers. If you get in their way, they can kill you, your friends, and any family that ask questions about your death. They can shut down the whole investigation by calling in few favors here and there."

"If you're trying to scare me, you succeeded. But guess what?"

"The only reason they are taking their time in killing me is because I'm in the big league. If I die, a lot of people will ask questions. That's why they're taking their time — so it doesn't come back to them."

"Guess what? You succeeded. I believe you. They are dangerous, and danger kind of gets me excited."

"Mara!"

"You haven't told me what happened after the wedding."

He ran his fingers through his hair in frustration. He had never known a woman as stubborn as this woman. Once her mind was set on doing something, there was nothing anyone could do about it. He alone ever came close to changing her mind in the past. But then, he couldn't complain. The fact that she was a woman who knew what she wanted was one of the reasons he was attracted to her in the first place.

"After the wedding," he continued, "I wasn't happy. Not for one day. Things got worse when I found out about her affair with the gardener. The boy's family threatened to press charges. I had to pay them off to shut down the case. After that, I decided I couldn't continue to be unhappy. I told Dahlia that I wanted a divorce. Not long after that, I started feeling sick. Inexplicable stomach pain, dehydration, fatigue. I tried many doctors, but none of them could figure out what was wrong with me. In the end, they put me on a medication that cured the symptoms, and I was able to go about my daily life. But even as I did, I knew that death was imminent. And I didn't want to die an unhappy man. So I went looking for my happiness. You, Mara. My happiness is you. I came looking for you. I only used my divorce as an excuse to see you."

"If you were alright—if you weren't sick—would you have come back for me?"

He knew Yes would have pleased her ears. Yes would have been the appropriate answer. But that wasn't him. He'd rather tell the truth. "Being sick—the fear that I might die any minute—gave me the strength and the courage to stand before you. Would I have come back for you if I wasn't sick? Maybe, maybe not. I don't know. All I know is I don't know how to live without you. That one year without you was hell."

He waited for her response. It took her longer than a second to respond, and when she did, she changed the subject. "I'll do everything I can to make sure Dahlia and the rest of them don't succeed." She let out a breath and continued. "I have work tomorrow. I have to go to bed." Her voice was soft and weak. She was understandably tired after a long day.

"Okay," he replied.

Hearing her sleepy voice made him imagine what she must be wearing. Her pink nightie? No, her silky, sheer, white nightie. If he was there with her, they'd have hot, steamy sex late into the night. And then she would fall asleep in his arms, and he'd stay awake longer, watching over her, listening to her steady breathing…

"Hang up, Ray…"

"Shhh! Be quiet. I'm listening to your breathing. I'm thinking about your steady breath after sex."

He could hear her breathing getting heavier. For one long second, no one said anything. Even in silence, Raymond felt as though he could hear her loudly, all the things she wanted but did not say.

"I wish you were here," she said, her voice needy. "I want to do some bad things to you right now."

"Hmm…" he smiled, biting his lower lip as he did. "I thought you wanted us to take a break from the relationship."

"Shut up, Ray! Good night."

He laughed. "Good night, baby."

EIGHT

Tamara was having a hard time concentrating on her driving. Her mind kept going back to Raymond's warning. He said those people were dangerous. If they found out that she was on to them, they could kill her and her entire family. She'd die because she was trying to save Raymond. And Mama always said, *Tamara, if you die because of a man, several tall, dark and handsome men will spit at your grave.* It was too complicated to understand at the time, but as she grew, she understood it perfectly. It means don't put yourself in harm's way just to hold on to a man. There are other men out there who will make you happy.

But this wasn't just about Raymond. She liked solving puzzles. And she might not know just when to stop.

Tamara pulled up to Sherry's house and got out of the car. With Drake gone, she needed her back. Walking to the front door, she pressed the doorbell and waited. A few seconds later, the door opened.

"Hi, Sherry," Tamara said.

Sherry held the door open and shot her a glare. "What do you want?"

"You're angry. I get it."

"Yes, I'm angry. You fired me! I pleaded with you."

Tamara stood still, a flash of angry intolerance burning in her brown eyes. Her voice came across very low, but harsh. "Let's get something straight. You're not in the position to be angry right now. First, you betrayed me. Second, because you'd be stupid not to recognize an opportunity when you see one."

"What opportunity?

"You are unfired. Come back to work."

Sherry swore softly and looked away, folding her arms across her chest and deepening her glare in a gesture she inherited from Tamara. "No! I'm not coming back."

Tamara's lips curved into a sly smile. "You amaze me."

"What's so funny?"

The smile disappeared from her face. "You see, Sherry, you're good at what you do. I see potential in you, and you will make a good lawyer one day. But you not only want to be a lawyer, you want to be like me. That is why, right now, you're folding your arms across your chest and glaring, just like I do when I try to show someone an attitude."

Gently, Sherry unfolded her arms and withdrew her glare.

"You are looking into my eyes and studying them. Just like me! The whole of your speech, your punctuations... you sound just like me. And it's not a bad thing to want to be like someone. But if you come back to work, you will learn not only to be a better lawyer but also be yourself. You have thirty seconds to decide if you want to come back or not. Thirty seconds!"

"You win! I'm in."

That brought a smile from Tamara, but it quickly faded. "Good! Now go back inside, get dressed, and let's go to work."

Sherry raised a brow. "Like, right now?"

"Hell, yeah."

She hesitated a while and said; "Okay. Come inside and wait for me."

"No, I'll wait right here."

"You sure?"

Tamara smiled. "Yes. I'll be fine."

Sherry closed the door and went back inside. Tamara hadn't waited longer than a minute when her phone rang. It was Megan.

She clicked the green button. "Megan?"

"Tamara, you have to be here right now. We have a client. This couple…"

"Handle it, Megan. I'm doing something right now."

"Tamara, I don't know…"

"I'm doing something," she broke in. "I'll be there in the next thirty minutes, but go ahead and handle the case."

"I can't do it. Tamara, you have to be here. Come and do what you do best. Talk some sense into their heads."

"Yes, Megan, you can. You've been with me how many years now?"

"Two or three years, I'm not sure. But that doesn't matter. Just COME HERE." She emphasized the "come here" to let her know she meant it.

"No, Megan, talk to the client. What if I'm not here? What if I'm out of town?"

"Yay! But you're not out of town, so come here."

"No. Go ahead and talk to the client. Bye."

"Tamara!"

She hung up.

A few seconds later, Sherry came out of the house wearing a light blue shirt over a short black skirt.

"That was quick," Tamara said.

"Well, how could I take my time dressing up when my boss is standing outside my house waiting for me?"

"That's the purpose."

Sherry's brow went up. "You intentionally stood outside just so I would hurry up?"

Tamara feigned a smile and began to walk toward her car. "I need you to do something for me."

Teetering on her heels, Sherry followed. "You said you came back for me because I'm good at my job."

Tamara stopped and turned to look at Sherry, a grin spreading across her face. "You didn't actually believe me when I said that, did you?"

"What?"

Tamara resumed walking to her car. "I need you to start walking for Dahlia again."

Sherry followed. "You know you could have just pleaded with me to come back instead of throwing those nice harsh words at me."

"Number one lesson you have to learn, Sherry. There are times you plead, and times when you use harsh words. And sometimes you manipulate with nice words. If you are smart, the times when you manipulate should be more than the times you plead."

Tamara went for the driver's seat as Sherry eased herself into the passenger's seat. "I want you to start working for Dahlia again," she repeated.

"You don't mean it, right? You're joking."

"I'm not laughing."

"What is going on here?" Sherry asked, her brow knitted in confusion. "First, you fire me because I was blackmailed into working for Dahlia, and now you hire me back because you want me to work for Dahlia."

"In a game, the best players don't play the cards. They play their opponents. That is why you're going to tell Dahlia about every step that I take. First, you're going to convince Dahlia that you haven't been compromised. I don't know that you're working for her. Second, you're going to convince Dahlia that I didn't tell Raymond that she is responsible for the arsenic poisoning."

Sherry flashed a big smile, arms flailing in excitement. "This is going to be fun."

"Well, I can't say it's going to be fun, but I know it's going to be interesting."

Tamara smiled at her, and then pulled onto the street.

****

"Where's the client?" Tamara asked as she walked into the lobby.

"Like you said, I'm more than capable of handling her. And I did."

Tamara smiled proudly, her full lips tightened and pushing back her cheeks. "I'm proud of you." The smile disappeared very quickly. "Both of you wait for me in the conference room. I'll be there in a second."

Megan looked at Sherry, and then exchanged a quick glance with Tamara. "Pardon me for asking, but what is Sherry doing here?"

"Oh! I forgot to mention. Sherry is unfired!"

"Really..."

Tamara had stopped paying attention. She walked speedily to her office, grabbed a folder and headed to the conference room.

Megan and Sherry were settled in their chairs when Tamara placed the folder on the table, sank gently into the armchair and rested her elbows on the table.

"Raymond tested positive for arsenic poisoning." Glancing at them, she saw the surprise on Megan's face. Opening the folder, she took out some documents and handed one to each of them. "That's the result of the test and also the transcripts of the recordings of my conversation with Dahlia."

Megan read through the documents very quickly, and with the softest voice, said, "Tamara, I'm sorry."

"Don't be," she replied. "I don't need your sympathy. What I need is your help in saving Raymond. Dahlia said she will finish the job on or before the wedding anniversary party, which is less than 72 hours from now. Help me to save Raymond

Connor." She glanced at the both of them. "But before you decide to help me, let me warn you. The people we are dealing with are wealthy, powerful and ruthless. They can kill and get away with it. I just want to make sure that you know what you're getting into."

She hated to finish in this manner, but she had to make sure that everyone understood the risks.

Megan shifted in her seat, her back hard and stiff. "We're in."

"And we know what we're getting into," added Sherry.

A faint smile curved Tamara's lips as she relaxed her back on the armchair. "So where do we start?"

"Looks like you got everything done already," Sherry replied. "You have the test results and Dahlia's confession. We take it to the police, and we let them do their job."

Megan rolled her eyes at Sherry. "Give a lazy woman a hard job, and she will find an easy way to get it done."

"I'm not lazy!" Sherry yelled.

Before Megan could respond, Tamara interrupted. "Stop!" she yelled, and then glanced at Sherry. "First, Raymond doesn't want the police involved. And second, the people that are using Dahlia might have friends inside the police department. So, for now, we take care of it ourselves. We will go to the police when we have enough evidence."

"If these people are as powerful as you say they are, they can get away even if we have enough evidence."

"Not if we have 'enough' enough evidence. Plus, I've got some friends in the police department, too. Ones I can trust. They won't let themselves be manipulated, bribed, or threatened into letting a criminal walk away. But I need enough evidence before I can ask them for help. So the question still is, where do we start?"

The room went dead silent. Tamara knew her clock was ticking. Whatever she needed to do, it had to be now, or else she might not be able to expose the people using Dahlia. And if she couldn't, she'd better be prepared to lose Raymond to death.

Sherry's voice broke through her thoughts. "Maybe we're taking this too serious. Maybe it's just very simple."

"What do you mean?" Tamara asked.

"Maybe, just maybe, all the killing is about the Connor wealth..."

Megan interrupted. "We know that already."

"Then we should be investigating people who have the right to inherit the Connor wealth if Raymond dies."

Realization flickered in Tamara's eyes. It jolted her, and she was angry at herself for not having thought of that. "Joe Connor, Josh Connor, Lisa Connor and Ben Murray," she said, almost like she was talking to herself. And then suddenly she glanced fiercely at Megan. "Do you still have the list of the fifteen people who knew about Raymond being a Connor before the rest of the world knew?"

"Yes, I do. Why?"

"Let me have it."

Megan walked out of the conference room and returned after a few minutes with a folder. Placing it on the table in front of Tamara, she said, "Here you go."

Tamara opened the folder and read through very quickly. "Ben Murray is not on the list."

"Next page," Megan said.

Tamara flipped to the next page and read though. She bit at her lips in anger. "How could I not have thought of this?"

Confused, Sherry and Megan glanced at each other, and then back at Tamara. "Hey, Tamara, you lost us. Tell us what's going on." Megan said.

Grabbing a paper, Tamara wrote down the four names she had previously spoken. "These four people," she said, showing them the names she had penned, "could also have been the Chairman of Connor Corp if James hadn't chose Raymond."

"But who is Ben Murray?"

"The vice chairman of the board of directors of Connor Corp. He also could have become the chairman after James Connor died. He has enough shares, enough experience, and 25 years of service to Connor Corp, but James Connor refused to give Connor Corp to him. He gave it to Raymond because, no matter what, James still thinks of Connor Corp as a family business."

"So Ben Murray! We have our guy," Sherry said.

Tamara shook her head. "No. We have four suspects."

NINE

Tamara clicked on the remote control, and the picture came on screen. "That's Joe Connor," Tamara said, pointing the remote at the screen, "the son of James Connor. When James named Raymond as heir to Connor wealth, Joe was furious. He went into a lengthy legal battle with Ray. I represented Ray, and we won the war. In the end, Joe settled his rift with Ray, and they both run Connor Corp together."

Tamara pressed the remote and another picture slid to the screen. "Josh Connor, the last son of James Connor. Has always shown no interest in Connor wealth. He moved to Europe a long time ago."

Tamara stopped talking as her eyes went briefly to Sherry. Her concentration was on the screen, and it seemed as if she wasn't aware of her surroundings. For a brief moment, Tamara studied her. "Sherry, are you here?"

Sherry placed both her palms on her chest as if trying to stop her heart from jumping out, staring wide-eyed at the screen as her jaw almost dropped on the floor. "OH. MY. GOSH. He's so damn HOT!"

Tamara lifted an eyebrow. "Who is hot?"

"Josh Connor," Sherry said, pointing to the screen.

Tamara stifled a laugh. When she couldn't hold it in any longer, she laughed out loud. The laugh became contagious as Megan joined in.

"What's so funny?" Sherry asked.

"Your face," Megan replied. "You look like a virgin girl who just saw the man who is going to be her first."

Sherry frowned and tossed her hair over her shoulder. "Whatever."

Tamara knew they were being unfair, always picking on Sherry. She didn't know why, but Sherry reminded her of the little sister she never had.

"Let's be serious," Tamara said, and shifted her concentration back to the screen. "Josh Connor graduated from Cambridge University with a Bachelor in English, but his interest lies in sports. Soccer to be specific."

"Do you have a cell number for him?" Sherry asked. "Or maybe you could ask Raymond if he does."

Tamara shot her a glare. "Sherry!"

Sherry continued looking at Tamara, her eyes pleading with her. "Please?"

"There's a life at stake here, so concentrate!" Tamara yelled.

Sherry murmured under her breath. "Concentrating would be easy if I didn't have to keep looking at his sexy picture on the screen."

"Don't forget the rules! You can't be sexually involved with a client…"

Sherry cut her off. "You broke that rule already."

The warning look Tamara shot Sherry felt like a scolding, and she stopped talking immediately. But her words struck Tamara like a blow to her throat, and her voice caught for a brief moment. She had nothing to feel bad about, she told herself. Sherry's words were true. She broke the rules, got involved with a client and threw all of their lives into a hot mess. When she finally found her voice, she continued with the presentation, her face deadly serious, never giving any sign of emotion. It rarely did.

"Josh Connor's interest is soccer. He plays for the Bebe football club. He's won best footballer of the year twice, back to back. He is worth millions of dollars, making all his money from sports. He presently lives in Spain. He has shown no interest and no ties to Connor wealth, and we could likely cross him off our suspect list."

She pressed the remote again. "Lisa Connor, wife of James Connor, mother of Joe and Josh Connor. Was very supportive of her husband's business, and could well have become the owner of Connor Corp."

She pressed the remote again. "And lastly, Ben Murray, vice chairman of the board of directors of Connor Corp. He could also have become the chairman after James Connor died. He has enough shares, enough experience, and 25 years of service to the company."

"So now that we know our suspects, what do we do?" Megan asked.

"We find anything that will connect them to Dahlia. Emails, call records, bank statements."

Megan stood up. "We still have Dahlia's phone records and bank statements, I'll get them."

Tamara nodded. "Okay," she said, and then faced Sherry. "Please get me a cup of coffee."

"Sure."

As soon as Megan and Sherry walked out of the room, Tamara took her phone and made a quick call to Joe Connor. It was strange that she was calling him, but she needed to know what kind of relationship he had with Raymond.

"Hello, Tamara," came his deep baritone voice. "To what do I owe this pleasant surprise?"

Tamara smiled, walking closer to the window and glancing out to the street. "How is me calling you a surprise?"

"Come on, Tamara. You and I don't see eye to eye, remember? You are either intimidating me to silence or yelling at me to silence. And the times you aren't doing either, you're accusing me of being involved in a conspiracy to kill my brother."

"I disagree. I think we don't get along because you still hate me for helping Raymond win the case that took your inheritance away."

"Talk of the blunt she-devil," he replied, taking the edge of his remark with a low laugh.

Tamara laughed. "Devil to the bad guys and an angel to the good."

"I still think Raymond is the only one that ever saw the angelic side of you."

"Trust me, Raymond sees both every day."

He laughed. "Still, you must have called me for a reason."

"Of course. I've been trying to call Raymond, and he hasn't been answering his phone," she lied. "So I decided to call you to check if you knew what's up with him."

"I think he's in the middle of a meeting with the board. Maybe call him in an hour or two. Or just go ahead and call Anita, his assistant. She knows more about his whereabouts than I do."

"Okay. Thanks."

"Glad to help."

Before she could hang up she heard Joe again. "Tamara, I think you and I need to meet and have a long talk."

Her suspicion flared anew. "Why?"

"Because I'm Raymond's brother. I'm the one you should be trying to impress if you really want be Mrs. Connor."

It brought a small smile to her face, but it quickly disappeared. "Impress you? That will be only in your dreams!"

He gave another of his low laugh. "But, seriously, you and I need to talk. It's about Raymond, I'm worried about him. He's sick. He told me you introduced him to a doctor, but I still think he's not taking care of himself enough."

Tamara heard the door open, and she quickly interrupted Joe. "I agree. We need to talk, but I've got my hands full right now. I'll let you know when I'm free. Once again, thanks for your help. Bye."

She didn't wait for his response. She hung up and walked away from the window.

"Your coffee," Sherry said, holding it out for Tamara.

Tamara didn't take the cup of coffee when Sherry handed it to her. She just stared at it as if she had forgotten ever asking Sherry for a cup of coffee.

"I don't want coffee," Tamara said, without paying the slightest attention to Sherry or the coffee.

Sherry frowned, a hint of irritation spreading across her face. "You asked for it."

Megan walked closer to Tamara and handed her a folder. "I got the call records and the statement of account."

Tamara didn't take the folder from her. "You mean the same call records and bank statements that we used when we were trying to save their marriage?"

Megan nodded.

"No, we can't find anything on there. These people are smart. They will cover their tracks."

Sherry interrupted. "But you told her to go get them. Seems like you intentionally got us out of the room."

Tamara put both her hands on her waist and glanced at Sherry. "I asked both of you for help, but I will be damned if I don't try to protect both of you. So the less you know, the safer you are."

She wasn't lying. She meant every word she said. And even though they knew what was at stake when she asked them for help, she still felt responsible for their safety.

She studied their faces for a brief moment to make sure they understood her. When she was sure, she withdrew her gaze and began to pace back and forth. A lot was going through her mind. From her conversation with Joe, it seemed he and Raymond got along okay. In fact, he sounded as if he cared about Raymond. She could as well cross him off the suspect list. Besides, Joe wasn't that smart. He was too stupid to actually think and orchestrate a conspiracy to kill a rat, let alone a human being.

Still pacing, she began to talk to no one in particular. "We need to follow Dahlia and know what she's up to between now and the anniversary. We need to get our hands on their secret emails, secret phone records, their secret 'secret' bank accounts…"

"Secret bank accounts?" Sherry asked.

Tamara shot her a suspicious glare. "You know something."

"I don't know if it's something."

Tamara walked closer, searching her eyes as if capable of finding the truth just by looking. "Tell me anyway."

Her voice was shaky. "Dahlia didn't start out by blackmailing me. She first tried to give me some money, but when I wouldn't do her bidding, she turned to blackmail." She paused and took a quick look at Tamara.

Tamara's face was expressionless. She would probably be unable to know what Tamara was thinking. "The money she tried to give me… it was $3,000."

Megan cut her off. "Eww! You betrayed Tamara for just $3,000?"

Tamara folded her arms, and her grin came back as she eyed Megan. "Judas betrayed Jesus for less. I'm glad she had the courtesy of taking that much."

Sherry scowled. "I didn't take the money. I gave it back to her!" she yelled.

Tamara smacked her shoulder playfully. "You can't take a simple joke."

"Dahlia transferred $3000 to my account," Sherry continued, "but I noticed something. The account the money came from wasn't in Dahlia's name."

Tamara edged closer to her. "Who owns the account?" she asked impatiently.

"Richard Connor."

****

Richard Connor was Raymond Connor's seven-month-old son.

What kind of mother was Dahlia? What kind of mother would commit a crime in her baby's name?

She had always known Dahlia to be smart, a woman who would go to any length to get what she wanted. But this was over the top. Not just over the top, it was stupid, because using an account in her son's name to pay for her bad deals would obviously lead back to her. And Dahlia wasn't that stupid.

Something just wasn't right. But Tamara couldn't place her hands on it yet. A lot of things weren't just right. The fact that the account was registered as Richard Connor and not Richard Brock was suspicious. Raymond had only changed his name to Connor a few days ago when the world found out who he really was. And going by Sherry's confession, the account had been in use long before that.

The more Tamara thought about it, the more complicated it seemed.

Tamara paced while Megan and Sherry sat, watching her, looking slightly uncomfortable. Suddenly, Tamara halted and strode over to them.

"Sherry," she called, her voice tense. "I have to know what Dahlia is doing every second, every minute from now until the anniversary party. I don't know how you're going to do it. Manipulate her, plead with her, suck her ass or follow her around. I don't care. I need results!"

Sherry nodded. "On it."

Tamara glanced at Megan. "And you, I want to know who is on Dahlia's payroll. I'd appreciate it if you could get me a statement of that Richard Connor account."

Megan gave her a worried look. "That's too much. That kind of record is something only the Feds have access to. Even if we can get our hands on them, this is not something I'm good at. This is Drake's job. We need him if we're going to actually pull this off."

Tamara stood straight, her back stiff. "Drake is not here anymore. Do what you can!"

"You don't get it, Tamara." Megan stood up to meet Tamara's height. "To get our hands on this without Drake, I'll have to break through several laws and protocols, blackmail, bribery..."

Tamara cut her off. "I don't care. If you have to bribe them all, do it!"

"We don't have that kind of money. We're talking about thousands and thousands of dollars."

Sherry cleared her throat to get their attention. "Excuse me. If I may…"

Tamara looked sharply at her. "What?!"

"Um…" she started slowly, afraid of the outburst that might follow her statement. "Bribery is a crime."

"Yes, it's a crime," Megan replied. "That's why we make sure we don't get caught."

"But…"

Ever heard about the end justifying the means? Tamara thought, but she was in no mood to argue with Sherry.

"Sherry, please, not now," was all she said, taking her concentration back to Megan. "How much do we have right now?"

"Some of our clients still owe us, but right now, we have about $20,000 to spare."

"Good. Start with that."

"We're going to be broke."

"You don't have to bribe everybody. Tell some people we're going to save their marriage for free, manipulate some others. Just do something."

"Tamara!"

"Megan," she said. She was about two inches taller than Megan and had to lower herself a little to meet her height. Resting her hands on the table, she looked Megan in the eyes. "I will figure something out, get us more money, but…" She began to jab one finger on the table repeatedly. "I need to get my hands on those records. I want to know the people on Dahlia's payroll."

TEN

Raymond Connor added his signature to the last of the stack of documents his assistant had piled on his desk. Slamming his pen on top of the stack, he pulled at his tie and leaned back in his leather chair, wondering how long he could keep up with all these lies and pretense with Dahlia, the secrets he kept from Mara, the threats on his life, and most important of all, the tension between him and Mara.

No comfort of her soft body wrapped around him. No kisses. No sex. No touching.

Mara had everything on hold.

It wasn't her fault.

But Raymond wondered if she knew she didn't have to do that to get him to be with her. She didn't have to withdraw all intimacy just to make him choose her. His heart had chosen her already. There wasn't even a choice. It was either Mara or Mara. Only Mara. There could be no one else.

But he understood her. He understood that she didn't want to continue to give herself to him while he was married to someone else.

That was why he started taking action. He was going to hold his end of the deal—find a way for them to be together without hurting Mara's career and let Mara take care of the people trying to kill him.

He knew what she was capable of. She was more than capable of unraveling the mystery behind the conspiracy to kill him. Still, he was going to try and make her job easier. He hired seven bodyguards to protect himself and no matter how much he hated it, he knew normal was over him.

He had stopped eating at home without raising Dahlia's suspicions.

As he relaxed in his enormous leather chair, he smiled to himself. This would end well. He would live happily ever after with Mara.

He smiled again because he knew his plan would work. Opening one of his desk drawers, he took out a folder and read through all the documents to make sure everything was intact.

When he heard a slight knock, he glanced at the door to see who it was. "Anita!"

"Yes, sir," she replied as she sashayed into the office. She went straight for the stack of documents on the table. "If you're done signing these, I'll take them now."

"Yes, please."

With both hands, she lifted the documents off the table. They were a little heavy, and she had to balance them on her chest for support.

"When you're done working on all of those, I want you to work on this one, too," he said as he handed her the folder containing the documents he had been reading through.

She didn't take it from him. "What's that?"

He continued to hold it out for her. "You know the building directly opposite Connor Corp?"

"The one that had 'For Sale' pasted on it?" she asked.

"Yeah."

"What about it?"

"This document contains everything you need to know about that building. I want you to close the deal. We're buying the building."

"You know what? I'm tired," she said. Dropping the stack of documents on the table, her hands reflexively rested on her waist. "I think we need to define what my job is. You can't have me running all the errands. There's a department here at Connor Corp that deals with acquiring new properties. Why should I add that to my job?"

"Because you're my personal assistant, and this is personal." He gestured for her to read the document.

Anita read through the document very quickly. When she finally glanced back at Raymond, her face had a hint of surprise and happiness. She leaned over a little, searching his eyes. "You're going to buy this for Tamara?"

He nodded proudly, smiling.

"It's going to cost about five million dollars."

He shrugged with a gentle smile. "It doesn't matter. Mara is worth more than that."

A grin spread across her face. "She's a lucky woman. And she's a wonderful woman, too, a rare gem."

"So you're going to help me?"

"Of course I am. You know I'm always interested in the matters of your heart."

"Thanks."

She dropped the document on the stack she had before and lifted it. "Anytime," she replied and began to walk out of the room.

When she got to the door, however, Raymond's voice brought her to a halt. "And it's nice to have your rude-self back, because your frequent use of SIR was beginning to get on my nerves."

"I'm sure you enjoyed it while it lasted." She smiled, opened the door and walked out, closing the door after her.

A few seconds later, the door opened again.

"Anita, you…" The rest of the words caught in his throat when he glanced at the door and realized it wasn't Anita. He took a good look at the woman standing before him. He remembered her. Sherry Mandy. She worked for Mara. She was almost as tall as Mara, dark-skinned with straight long hair, and probably in her mid-twenties.

"Is it a bad time? Your secretary said I could come in. I'm sorry."

"You're fine. I wasn't expecting a visitor."

Walking toward him, she held out a hand in greeting. "Hello, Mr. Connor."

"Hi, Sherry," he replied as they shared a handshake. "You can call me Raymond." He pointed to the chair opposite him. "Please, sit."

Cautiously, she sat on the armchair. Her eyes constantly roamed around the office as if she were fascinated by it.

"Do you want something to drink?" he offered.

She smiled. "No, I'm fine. Thanks."

She glanced around again, the expression on her face indicating that she liked what she saw. "WOW! Your office is beautiful. I mean... um... it's large... and... nice decor," she stuttered to a halt. "I mean, not that I expected any less... but... um..."

"Thank you, Sherry," he said with a gentle smile. "Shouldn't you be at work by this time of the day?"

Her face turned deadly serious. "What I'm here to tell you, please, you must not tell Tamara. If she finds out, she will roast me alive."

He played along. "Tell me what the problem is. I won't tell her."

She leaned closer and lowered her voice. "We're broke. Not that we're 'broke' broke, but we need some documents to help with your case, and it's going to cost a lot of money to get it. Tamara promised to get some money, but I can see she is really troubled about it. And I hate to see her like that. So I think..."

He broke in. "You think it's my case, and I should be able to fund it."

She leaned back and nodded gently. "I guess she didn't want to ask you because she didn't want it to seem like she's doing all this for you because she's interested in your money."

That sounded exactly like Mara. She wouldn't take a penny of his money. He had wanted to provide her everything—the best car, the best house. He wanted to make her the envy of every woman. He could afford it. God knows he had the resources. But Mara wouldn't take anything from him. Not that he ever had any question about her being a gold digger. In fact, everything he had to this day, he had because Tamara helped fight for it.

He leaned back with a frustrated sigh, and then he glanced at Sherry. "Thanks, Sherry. I'll handle it."

Sherry nodded. "Thanks, but please don't tell Tamara I was here."

He placed a palm over her hand and looked re-assuringly into her eyes. "Trust me, I won't say anything to Mara."

****

Tamara had a lot of catching up to do. Ever since she started working on Raymond's case, she had almost forgotten about her other clients. Not that she was ready for them anyway. At this moment, she could think of nothing else except making sure Dahlia didn't succeed.

Megan had been dealing with the other client.

The only thing left for Tamara to do was to read through the report and make sure Megan did a perfect job.

And that was what she had been doing. Every now and then, her mind would slip back to Raymond's case. How was she going to come up with the money to get this done? It wasn't only the money that bothered her. She was supposed to be a symbol of morality. How could she endorse getting things done through bribery? The last she remembered, bribery was still a crime in the United States.

Not only that, it was unethical—but she had no other choice.

Unless Drake would come back. He knew people in the right places.

Her eyes went to the door as she heard a light knock. Megan walked in.

"Tamara, you did it!" Megan said, excitement written all over her face and voice.

Tamara's brow wrinkled in confusion. "Did what?"

"I checked the firm's account, and we have $60,000 more."

Tamara's eyes went wide.

"I thought you had something to do with it."

"Who made the deposit?"

Megan hesitated for a short while. "Connor Corp."

Anger flared in her eyes. "Of course, I had something to do with it." Reaching for her purse, she stood up and walked fiercely out of her office.

She could hardly contain her anger as she drove speedily to Connor Corp. A few minutes later, she pulled up at the parking lot of Connor Corp and walked hurriedly into the building.

"Hi, Tamara, how are you doing?' said Anita.

"I'm doing alright." She feigned a smile, but the smile disappeared very quickly. "Is he in?"

"Yes, but…"

Tamara ignored the rest of her statement and began to walk toward Raymond's office. Anita caught up with her and threw herself in front of her. "You can't go in. Not now. He's having an important meeting with the board of directors. Maybe if you wait for..."

Tamara scowled. "I have to see him now!" She didn't realize she was close to yelling.

ELEVEN

Mara!

That was Mara's voice.

Raymond was certain of it.

He could recognize that voice in his sleep.

"Please, give me a few minutes. I'll be right back." He excused himself from the meeting and immediately stepped out.

"Mara!" he called. She looked toward him, and when he saw the expression on her face, he knew something wasn't right. She was angry about something, and he knew what it was. He glanced at Anita. "Leave us."

"Okay." Anita left.

He walked toward Tamara, one slow step at a time. When he was close to where she stood, he touched her shoulder very gently. "What's the problem, Mara?"

Her gaze went slowly from his hand on her shoulder up to his face. "Take your money back!"

He took his hand off her shoulder, sliding it into the pocket of his trousers. "No!" he replied, his tone adamant and inflexible. "You need that money and you will take it and spend it and do whatever you like with it."

She shook her head. "I don't need the money. We had an agreement, didn't we? If I'm ever in need of anything, I'll ask you, but I don't need this."

His expression softened a little. "Are you sure?"

"Absolutely."

He shrugged. "Okay, then consider the money as a payment for what you've been doing for me. You've said it over and over again that I'm your client. And clients pay, right?"

"Yes, but I planned to charge you only $10,000, and that's because you're rich. But $60,000? That's more than a little too much!"

He barked out a short laugh, devoid of humor. "How do you make profits? You're going to charge me $10,000, and it's going to cost you far more than that to get the documents that you need to get the case done."

Tamara raised a brow. "How do you know about that?"

"Sherry told me," he replied. "And I forbid you from saying anything to her," he quickly added. "The girl thinks you're going to roast her alive if you find out."

"Oh, I'm going to fry her alive. Does she know nothing about confidentiality?"

He smiled. "Please don't fry or roast her, but seriously… keep the money. You need it."

"We were trying to get some documents, and we might need to pay some people off before we can get our hands on them," she explained. "But I have another option, one that I wouldn't have to bribe to get what I want. You see, I don't need your money."

"Still, keep it."

"$60,000 is too much!"

"I am the owner of one of the most powerful corporations in the world. You do have the idea of how much is or is not too much for me, right?"

She cut him off. "Dammit, Ray," she growled. "I am not a damsel in distress that needs to be rescued by a lousy billionaire. I am not interested in your money. If you want to pay me for the work that I'm doing for you, $10,000 is what you owe. The rest of the money, I don't need. If you're giving me that much because of us—because you think somehow you owe me—you owe me nothing. I am not a whore that you can pay off. I am not a mistress that takes comfort in wealth when she can't have the real thing. And if it's just because you want to help me, you feel you can help me, well Mr. Billionaire, please wake up from your daydream, because this is reality. Billionaires don't just look for a damsel to squander their money on. That kind of thing only happens in the movies. So, wake up!"

"WOW! If that was to get me angry, you did it. But guess what? You're still going to keep the money." If Tamara was making this much noise over $60,000, he wondered what she would do when she found out about the office building he was going to buy for her.

"Ray!"

He pulled her to himself and held her tightly against himself. "We'll talk about this later. I'm in the middle of a meeting with the board."

She tried to push him away.

"Hey, hey," he said in a low voice. "I'm sorry. I know how you feel about taking money from me. I'm sorry if I came on too strong about it."

She stopped fighting and looked at him. "Does it mean you're going to take the money back?"

"No! Keep the money. I don't care what you do with it," he said in a tone that refused to be disobeyed.

"Ray!"

"Mara, I've lost more than $600,000 in the last five minutes talking to you." Almost immediately after the words fell from his stupid mouth, Raymond regretted it and wanted nothing more than to take them back.

Tamara's beautiful face fell, the intense hurt and anger showing in her watered eyes. "I'm sorry," she said and turned to leave.

But his strong hands stopped her, pulling her back and forcing her into his arms, holding her as tightly as he could.

She struggled a bit, but he wouldn't let go of her. He passed one hand around her waist and pulled her hard against his body, grabbing the back of her hair with his other hand and kissing her with hot, urgent and demanding kisses, fire burning through his veins.

She melted into the kiss, her heart racing in her chest.

He broke off the kiss. Heads touching, he looked at her. It took her more than a second before she opened her eyes. And when she did, she was looking hungrily into his eyes as she swallowed hard.

They had not made love in a long time and the spark between them quickly ignited, sending fire through their veins.

"Tonight. Your place," he said.

It wasn't even a question.

But she answered anyway.

"Tonight. My place."

****

As Tamara got into the car and started the engine, she knew as surely as the sun rose in the east each morning that she'd missed him.

She'd missed Raymond too much.

They had grown apart lately. Because she wanted to take a break from the relationship. Because she was trying to do the right thing. Because she thought it was wrong to keep sleeping with a married man no matter what the circumstances were. Because she wanted to take a break.

Take a break, my ass!

She decided there and then that she was done fighting herself. For once in her life, she was going to go after what she wanted without thinking about right and wrong. Just like Raymond always said, *When it comes to you, Mara, there is no right or wrong. There is just you and me.*

As she parked in her garage, a tiny voice in her head brought her thoughts to a halt, telling her she had work to do if she wanted to keep seeing Raymond alive.

If she must get things done, she needed Drake. Nothing was ever going to change that. Reaching for her cellphone, she dialed his number very quickly. It rang, but he didn't pick up. She tried again. And then again. He finally picked.

"Hey, Drake," she said.

"Why are you calling?" he asked, his voice low and husky.

"Just checking up on you."

"Well, I've not been drunk. I've not been arrested by the police. And I've certainly not committed suicide. So, thanks for calling."

"Drake, please, come back," she pleaded.

"I'm not coming back," he answered, his tone adamant. "I'm hanging up now!"

"Wait! Um…" She stuttered a bit, telling herself to summon the courage to be honest with him, just this once. "What happened between us, I was wrong, and you were right. You've been by my side all this while, and I took you for granted, but if it changes anything, I want you to know that there were times I saw you as something more than just a friend. I wanted us to be something more than just friends. I waited for you, too. You were always with other girls, and I thought maybe you felt nothing for me. In the process of waiting for you, I met Raymond." She paused to swallow the lumps in her throat. "I met Raymond, and it changed everything. Everything. Maybe if we get reborn in the next world, you and I might change fate and be together. But in this world, please, do not ruin the great friendship we've built all these years. Come back! I need you! The law firm needs you."

She stopped talking and waited for a response. Silence roared back into her ear. "Drake? Drake?

Are you there?" When she still didn't hear anything, she hung up.

She sucked in her breath and let it out gently.
And then she picked up her purse and got out of
the car.

When she got to the front door, she inserted her
key into the lock, opened the door and walked in.
Throwing her purse on the couch, she wanted to
take off her shoes and relax when she felt something icy and strong at the back of her head. When
she heard a click, she knew someone was holding a
gun to her head.

"Don't move!"

Dozens of emotions clashed through her — and
she just couldn't process any of them.

Fear took over her sense of self and sent goose
bumps running through the whole of her body.
Reflexively, she turned to look at her captor.

"Don't fuckin' move!" he said again.

And before she knew what was happening, her
legs were swept out from under her. In a nanosecond, her body crashed to the carpeted floor of her
house. A scream tore from her throat. She wanted
to get up, but couldn't. Strong hands pinned her
down as he tied her hands behind her and then
gave her feet the same fate.

It ended as quickly as it started. Rough hands
grabbed her, lifted her to her feet and helped sit on
the couch.

Standing behind the couch, he grabbed her hair
and twisted her head back until his face loomed
over hers.

Tears filled her eyes and rolled speedily down her cheeks. "It hurts," she said through clenched teeth.

"Do as I say and you might live." His voice was deep, almost gentle. However, the threat in it was as evident as daylight.

She tried to nod but his grip held her head in place. When she tried to right her head, the pain came back fresh and powerful. She thought she might pass out.

Tamara had never been in a situation like this before. She had seen them in movies and read them in books, but had never witnessed it before. She had always managed to stay out of trouble. She chose to specialize in family law just so she could avoid having anything to do with criminals or crime. But more and more, she'd been getting involved in things that were beyond her. Raymond warned her. He did. But the stupid, stubborn her wouldn't listen.

The man strolled slowly from behind the couch and stood right in front of her. She finally got the chance to take a look at him. He was tall, huge and his face was rough and handsome. If Tamara had to guess his age, she would say he was probably in his mid-twenties. How did a man so young get himself involved with this kind of mess?

Grabbing her purse, he fumbled through it until he found her cellphone. "I'm going to call Raymond Connor. And you're going to talk to him and calmly, gently and sexually invite him here."

He stared into her eyes, waiting for a response that indicated she understood him, but Tamara refused to respond. She stared back at him, her face blank, devoid of emotion.

His fierce brown eyes glared. "Do you understand?" he asked through gritted teeth, his voice harder.

Tamara swallowed hard.

Her heart felt as if it was coming into her throat, but she tried to sound strong and fearless. "I'm not used to receiving orders."

It took her only a nanosecond before she began to regret what she said. Because immediately after she said that, he glanced at her with fury. Putting all his strength into it, he slapped her hard across her face.

For a brief moment, Tamara could hear nothing in her environment. She felt deafened. A powerful headache threatened to split her head.

She felt helpless.

She was tied up. And even if she wasn't tied up, she couldn't help herself. She had no knowledge or skill in self-defense, and she didn't know how to fire a gun if she had one.

If she got out of this alive, she vowed to learn how to defend herself.

But this day, she needed to use her head instead of being stubborn.

"Why are you doing this?" she asked, her voice shaky. "Whatever they're paying you, it's not worth it."

He looked away and sighed. "Mom didn't fuckin' have time for me. Dad left me when I was young. I grew up on the street. Smoked weed, sold crack, did drugs and got into trouble." He walked closer to where Tamara sat.

When he turned to her, he pulled out a scary-looking curved knife. He leaned closer and gave a menacing smile that was as cold as a winter night. "Is that what you wanted to hear?" His smile broke into a loud laugh without humor. "You know, I was warned to be careful, that you might try to get into my head. And you did exactly as predicted."

He patted her shoulder with the knife. "Eventually, you will do as I say." His voice was hard and dangerous. "It depends on how much you want it to hurt."

The touch of the knife sent shivers down her spine, her breathing rapid.

Face close, he slowly placed the tip of the knife on her upper arm and slowly, ever so slowly, began to drag the knife downward, ripping her flesh open.

Blood rushed out in brooks, and her cry cut through the silence of the room.

Her whole body quivered from the pain. She felt weak, as if her very life was bleeding away.

Hastily, he cut out part of Tamara's blouse and wrapped it tightly over the wound to control the bleeding. Then he picked up Tamara's phone and held it close to her face. "You will talk to Raymond!" he growled.

Tamara nodded very quickly. She was helpless. The earlier she accepted it, the better. Resistance wouldn't do her any good.

He began to go through her contacts. "You got his cell number?"

"410..." she sobbed quietly. "264... 2155."

He dialed the number, turned on the speaker and held it closer to Tamara. It wasn't long before Raymond picked up the call. "Hey, Mara."

"Hey, honey," she replied. Yes, honey! She hardly called him that, but she was thinking if she said things she didn't usually say, maybe Raymond would figure out something was wrong.

"Are you okay?" he asked in a husky, concerned voice.

TWELVE

The meeting with the board of directors didn't end until 6p.m. Not that Raymond was paying attention any longer. All he could think about was Mara and the passionate kiss they had shared that afternoon—and how he couldn't wait to get home to finish what he started. Oh! And home was wherever Mara was.

At 6p.m., he was more than glad to bring the meeting to a close. He hurriedly packed his briefcase, said a quick goodbye to Anita and rushed out of the office. Stopping at Da Mimmo's Italian restaurant, he grabbed dinner for two. He already had everything planned in his head. He would stop at Mara's office, pick her up, and then they'd go home together. Although what he had planned with Mara was a sex date, he wanted to make everything special.

Sex date, hmm? It was just like the first time they met. Their love... it was love at first sex. He smiled to himself as the memory returned to him.

After parking his car, he strode into the building. He was just in the lobby when he heard his name.

"Raymond Connor?"

He glanced around to put a face to the voice that had just called his name. When he finally saw the person, he couldn't remember ever seeing the face. He was no movie star, but the series of events and the scandal in the news had kind of put his face out there, and he hated it. When all of this was over, he would crawl back into the hole he came from. He would stay away from the media. But he knew he would be in the media one more time when he made the announcement that would shock the day-light out of Mara and the whole world.

He smiled to himself as that crazy thought formed in his mind. Of course, the stranger assumed he was smiling at her.

She smiled back and extended a hand in greeting. "My name is Rosy Bloomington. I'm a client of Tamara Price."

"My name is Raymond Connor, and I'm a client of Tamara Price."

"Client, hmm?" she grinned as she winked at him. "Just so you know, I wanted it to be true when both of you were... you know... romantically linked together. I kind of rooted for the two of you..."

Raymond actually liked this woman. Anyone who loved him and Mara together had certainly gained a plus with him.

He smiled at her, genuinely this time.

Perhaps Sherry noticed it as she tried to throw in a word for Rosy. Sherry was becoming more like Tamara as each day passed.

"Mr. Connor, Rosy just got divorced and came to us to help fight for the custody of her daughter.

To win that fight, she needs a job and…" her voice gently fell off.

Raymond smiled and gave her a sidelong glance. "And you think maybe I could help."

She nodded.

Raymond glanced back at Rosy. "Work experience?"

"Yes," she replied very quickly. "I worked at BDTK. I was the secretary to…"

He cut her off. "Maybe you just got a job."

"WOW!"

"Not certain. I said maybe." He put his hand in the chest pocket of his suit and brought out a small business card.

"Your card?"

"No, my brother's. His name is Joe Connor. He's presently in need of a secretary. If you make as good an impression on him as you did with me, he might hire you."

"Wow! Thanks."

"And tell him that you came highly recommended." He grinned and winked at her.

"Thank you very much," she said again.

"Thank you," Megan and Sherry chorused.

"Anytime," he replied.

Megan looked at Rosy. "Well, that's it for tonight, Miss Bloomington. We'll see you again tomorrow."

Rosy nodded, smiling as she gave both Megan and Sherry a quick hug. She offered another heartfelt thank you to Raymond, and then was gone.

"It's late," Raymond said. "You should be home by now."

"We were just finishing with the client," Megan replied. "We'll be closing soon."

He nodded and then asked, "Mara here?"

Megan shook her head. "No. She left a few hours ago and didn't come back."

Before Raymond could respond, the front door opened. He glanced at the door to see who it was.

"Drake!!!" Megan and Sherry chorused. Sherry ran up to him and into his arms like a kid who was super happy that his parent was back after a long journey.

"Oh, Drake, it's nice to have you back."

Still in the hug, Drake rolled his eyes. "Your boobs grew bigger." His tone made it seem like a question.

Sherry quickly released herself from his hug and threw a playful punch at his shoulder. "You haven't changed."

He smiled.

Megan walked closer to him. "It's nice to have you back. I want to hug you, but not until you promise you won't be thinking about my boobs."

He shook his head. "Can't promise that."

"Okay." She extended a hand in greeting. "It's nice to have you back."

Drake took her hand and pulled her into his arms. Megan wrestled out of his arms and threw a punch at him.

"We've had peace ever since you left."

"You missed me," he said with an arrogant smile. And then he lifted his eyes and looked toward Raymond. "Raymond," he said as he walked toward him and they shared a greeting. "Where is Tamara?"

"She's not here," Raymond replied.

"She called me to come back. She said the law firm needs me!"

Megan snapped. "Whatever that is, it's going to be tomorrow. I have a husband who is waiting for me at home."

"I was just about to leave, too," Raymond said.

Almost immediately, his cell rang. He took it out and checked who it was.

"Hey, Mara."

"Hey, honey," she replied.

Honey? That was strange. Mara usually wouldn't say that. Who knows? Maybe she was trying to change. But it wasn't only the fact that she called him honey. There was something more. There was something in her voice that betrayed a troubled spirit.

"Are you okay?" he asked in a husky, concerned voice.

She hesitated a while. "Of course, I am. Why do you ask?"

"Your voice. You sound tired and different."

"Yes... I'm tired. I've been in the kitchen. Cooking. I hope you didn't forget about our date."

Mara! Cooking? Unbelievable!

"Of course, I didn't forget. I bought dinner at an Italian restaurant, but I'll gladly throw it in the bin for what you cooked."

"Don't expect too much of my cooking," she said with a smile in her voice. "Where are you, anyway? Don't keep me waiting for too long."

"I'm at your office, but I'll be at your place in a few."

"Megan and Sherry still there?"

"Yes."

"It's late. Tell them to go home. And please, tell Megan to email me the blue file before she leaves."

"Okay, baby. And don't stress yourself too much. You sound very tired. You can wait for me, and I'll come help with the cooking."

"Okay, baby. I'll be waiting for you. And please don't forget to tell Megan to email me the blue file. I want to work on it through the night."

"Alright. See ya in a few."

He hung up and glanced back at them. "I've got to run. Mara is waiting."

"Okay. Thanks for stopping by," Sherry said and gave him a light hug. "And thanks for helping Rosy."

"Anytime."

Drake extended a hand in greeting. "Thanks for stopping by, Man."

"Not a problem," he replied, and then glanced at Megan. "Oh! Megan, Mara wants you to email her the blue file. She wants to…"

"BLUE FILE!!!"

Drake and Megan yelled, horror in their voices.

Confused, Raymond exchanged a quick glance with Sherry. She seemed as confused as he was. And then he glanced back at Drake. "What's the blue file?"

Drake stiffened with a terrifying look. "Blue file is the code we designed for asking for help if you're in danger."

"If Tamara is asking for the blue file, she's asking for help," Megan added.

Raymond's body tensed and his muscles hardened. The thought that Mara could be in danger was almost driving him insane. Reasoning came back to his mind, and he understood Mara's hint. Calling him honey, telling him she was cooking... She was saying unusual things so he could know something wasn't right. Someone was making her call him. Someone was holding her hostage!

"Call 911! Now!"

If anything happened to Mara, he didn't know what would happen to him. He wouldn't forgive himself.

He hurried out of the office as Drake followed.

****

His uneasiness grew with each passing minute. He gave Tamara such a look of cold danger that it froze her where she sat. "Why is he not here?" he growled.

"I don't know," she replied. "You heard me talk to him. He'll be here."

He withdrew his look and began to pace back and forth in frustration.

"Whatever she is paying, it's not worth it," Tamara said.

Rushing to where Tamara sat, he pressed the gun to her forehead. "Shut up!"

She shuddered and tried to move. Her arms felt heavy, like they had been bruised badly. She fought the urge to scream in pain. "You don't have to do this."

"I said shut up!" he yelled.

She swallowed hard. "If you stop this now, I won't press charges. It would be as if this never happened. You can go on and enjoy your life."

"Enjoy? You don't know the first fuckin' thing about my fuckin' life."

"You're right, I don't know, but I do know that you're young and you have a bright life ahead of you... and you don't want to be a murderer!"

His brow drew down in a dark glare. "Shut the fuck up! And stay the fuck out of my head!" he growled in a way that gave Tamara an icy shiver and snapped her mouth closed.

Tamara knew she was getting to him and wanted to persist when her home phone rang. He glanced at the home phone and then back at her.

"Quiet," he said and walked to the phone. He put the phone on speaker and listened.

The voice came strong and firm. "This is Detective Lance. I'm with the Baltimore City Police Department. You have been surrounded..."

He dropped the call and rushed back to Tamara. "You called the police?"

She shook her head very quickly. "No. You tied my hands. You have my phone. I didn't call the police."

He pointed the gun at her again. "Shut up, bitch, and let me think."

Walking toward the window, he looked out into the streets. Blue and red lights flashed into his eyes. Five or six police cars were parked in front of the house. The police were heavily armed. He knew they wouldn't hesitate to gun him down should the need arise.

By the time he walked back to Tamara, he was jittery. He was scared and nervous to the bone. "FUCK!!!!!!!! It wasn't supposed to come to this. She said it wouldn't come to this," he said to himself as he paced back and forth. "Raymond was supposed to get here, not the cops. I'm supposed to kill both of ya. Make it clean. Like suicide."

"If you let me go, I can go out and tell the cops that it was a mix-up. You'll be free. I won't press charges."

"SHUT UP!!!" he yelled and rushed back to the home phone.

Tamara could not figure out what he was up to, but a few seconds later, she heard him talking on the phone. This time, he didn't put it on speaker.

"Detective Lance," he said. "Maybe we can reach an agreement. Send me Raymond Connor, and I'll give you Miss Price alive."

Cold dread ran through her and heat of panic rose in her. Tamara suddenly felt the need to yell. "NO!!!!!!!!!!!! DON'T!!!! DON'T!!!"

She knew Raymond was stupid enough to let himself be handed over. And they would both be dead. He wasn't going to let her live.

Before she knew what was happening, he charged toward her in a frightening rush; held her throat tightly and pinned her head to the couch.

"One more word and you're dead," he said.

Tamara tried to nod, but he hadn't released his hold on her neck. There was a savage anger in his brown eyes, and as she tried to breathe, breathing became more difficult. She knew she was about to die.

And then she heard the door open. Glancing at the door, her blurry eyes caught the frame of Raymond as he charged in a rush toward her captor. Raymond pushed him off her. As she tried to stay conscious, her terrified eyes looked for Raymond. It looked like he had engaged her captor in a fight. Darkness crawled into her vision as she struggled to stay awake, wondering if Raymond would be alright. If Raymond died, she could just as well surrender into the arms of death right now.

That was the last thing on her mind before she slid into complete darkness and an overwhelming silence.

THIRTEEN

Tamara Price opened her eyes slowly, blinking several times to clear her blurred vision. While she lay there, she took stock of her current condition. Her throat felt tightened. Her stomach was queasy. Her head pounded. And her arm throbbed below the makeshift bandage.

Tamara's memory returned slowly, bit by bit. Held hostage by a gunman. Ripping the flesh of her arm with that wicked, curved knife. Raymond came in…

Raymond! Was he okay? Was he alive?

Her eyes scanned the room. She was on a hospital bed. The bed next to her was empty.

Her throat was dry, and she would appreciate any liquid down her throat. She tried to reach for a cup of water on the bedside table. She flinched as she moved her hand, stretching the I.V. tubing inserted into the back of her hand, resisting the urge to cry out in pain.

Trying to lift her other hand to grab the cup of water, she discovered it was being held captive by a strong, large warm hand.

"Ray…" her voice came in a low whisper as she realized that she wasn't alone. Her eyes went straight to the hand, only to realize that her fingers were entwined in his, his head next to their entangled hands, his eyes closed.

He made it. He was alive!

Her heart melted a thousand times over as she watched him sleep, knowing how lucky she was. This man loved her to the point of sacrifice, to obsession—to the point of insanity. Jumping into harm's way because of her was insane.

He looked so peaceful in his sleep. Tamara wondered how long he'd been there. Her eyes went to the clock, and she could see that it was 6a.m. More than twelve hours had passed since the horrifying incident began.

Had he been here all night? Watching her, waiting for her to wake up, troubled that she might die? Had he ever left the hospital? He was still dressed in the same blue shirt he wore to work yesterday. He hadn't left her side.

Slowly, she tried to release her fingers from his so she could grab her cup of water. The act woke him up, and he jerked into a sitting position, his eyes focused on her and his hands reflexively bringing their hands together.

"Mara, thank God you're awake."

She could still feel the dryness in her throat. As she reached for the cup of water on the bedside table, Raymond sprang from his chair, unwrapped a straw and dipped it into the cup before bringing it to her lips. She took a long, slow sip until she was satisfied.

Raymond placed the cup on the table and took her hands in his again, his eyes fixed on her. "You almost died. I almost lost you. Don't you dare put me through that again."

She squeezed his hand. "I almost lost you too…"

"I'm going to put a security team on you. They will have to follow you and keep their eyes on you. I'm not letting this happen again."

She let go of his hand. "I don't need a security team. It's you they're after…"

"Dammit, Mara! Don't be an idiot." He scowled at her. "Now is not the time to be stubborn. I have bodyguards in place for me, and if they can't get to me, they'll come after you. If they get you, they got me already. You should know that by now."

She was quiet, and he was pissed as hell. But that was only because he was worried sick about her.

She looked at him, her voice low. "Don't be an idiot next time. Coming in to save me wasn't a good idea. You should have let the police do their job."

That eased the tension a little bit.

"I won't let anything happen to you," he said and placed a small, soft kiss on the back of her hand as his eyes locked with hers.

"I'm sorry I ruined our date."

He smiled. "I don't care about that. All that I care about is that you are okay."

She looked into his eyes a long moment. She didn't know what to say. Her only answer was a smile.

The moment passed, and she untangled her hand from his and asked gently, "Where am I?"

He told her the name of the hospital and explained that her CT scan was okay. The cut in her arm wasn't deep, and the doctor was only keeping her overnight for observation.

"So they're going to let me go today?" she asked anxiously.

He frowned. "Yes, but why are you so anxious to leave?"

"Ray, tomorrow night is your wedding anniversary party. I was attacked last night just because they want to get to you. Is it making sense yet? Looks to me that the countdown to your death has begun, and I'm not going to be sleeping here, doing nothing."

Raymond's body tensed and his chest vibrated with pure emotion. "I don't care about any countdown! Getting you involved was my mistake in the first place. From now on, you're going to stay out of this and let me handle it."

She was surprised by his agitation. "I was attacked last night. I'm involved already. You can't stop me!'

He shot her a dangerous glance. "We're not going to debate this. You're going to stay out of it," he said with a finality that irritated Tamara.

Before she could respond, the door opened and Sherry, Megan and Drake walked in. Raymond stood from the chair and stepped back a little so they could have access to Tamara.

Sherry and Megan dropped flowers on the bedside table before giving Tamara a hug. "I'm glad you're okay," Megan said as she took a seat beside Tamara on the bed.

Sherry sat at the other side of the bed. "We were scared to the bone. Raymond was really brave," she said, casting a quick glance at Raymond. He only gave a small smile.

Tamara smiled and glanced at Drake. "You came…"

He nodded gently. "I wouldn't miss seeing how ugly you look on a hospital bed. Wait, let me take a picture of you." He reached for his phone.

"No… don't…"

Few minutes later, they were chatting away, laughing easily together—all thanks to Drake and his jokes.

The moment passed and Drake changed the subject, his face serious. "Sherry and Megan brought me up to date on what we need for the case. I'll get it before the end of today."

Tamara took a quick glance at Raymond before she responded. His face warned her to give up on the case. Ignoring the subtle warning, she stared at him nicely. "Raymond, you've been here since yesterday. I think you can go home now and get some rest. I'll be fine."

It was obvious Raymond didn't like the idea, but Tamara was trying to get him off her back for when the doctor would release her—because she was going to do the exact opposite of his order.

"Okay," he finally agreed, and then glanced at Drake. "Drake, please look after her."

Drake nodded. "Of course."

He placed a quick, soft kiss on her lips before he left and immediately he stepped out of the room, Tamara glanced at Drake. "Drake, do you know if the police got any info from the guy who held me hostage?"

He shook his head sadly. "He didn't make it."

Tamara stared wide-eyed. "How? What happened?"

"The police got to the scene few seconds after Raymond engaged him in a fight. They told him to stand down, but he wouldn't. He shot at a cop. He gave them no choice…"

****

Drake had left the hospital to work on getting the documents. A few hours later, Tamara was discharged from the hospital, and the girls took her home. Surprisingly, she felt great. Only her arm hurt a little. And that was only because of the wound.

As soon as they all left, she headed straight to work. She knew the idea was crazy. Even though she felt okay, she still needed rest. But then her time was running out.

Drake later came to her house and gave him the bank records. When he and the girls left, Tamara went to her office. Alone.

Tamara's office was one of the few places where she could remain even close to uninterrupted. She could concentrate on whatever work came her way, free from the annoyances of daily life. No children ran down the halls screaming bloody murder, no domestic squabbles — no, only her and the hum of her laptop, and the occasional ringing of her phone.

However, today was not a simple day; it was plagued by an interruption that Tamara struggled to welcome with opened arms. It was tall, dark, handsome and named Raymond.

She tried to get him off her back, but that didn't work. He had gone back to the hospital to find out she was gone. He then checked her house before coming to look for her at the office.

The door to her office opened and he walked in, standing in the entrance as he set eyes on her. He wasn't at all in a good mood.

"You still won't give up," he said as he slowly walked toward her.

Honestly, he looked like he hadn't slept in days, with dark circles beneath his eyes and his handsome face marked with stress.

He was worried sick about her.

But he sure looked better than the last time she saw him at the hospital. He had at least had a bath, and she could smell his cologne. He smelled fresh and delicious.

"Giving up would mean giving up on you, and I can't do that."

He didn't try to argue with her. He just dropped his briefcase on the table and stood still, looking at her, towering over her.

Tamara disliked having to look up at him, so she stood up from her armchair and walked closer. "Ray, the wedding anniversary party is tomorrow."

He shrugged. "I know."

"I can't just sit here and do nothing."

"I know."

"Ray…"

He cut her off. "I'm not trying to stop you. That's not why I'm here."

She gave him a worried frown. "Then why are you here?"

Slowly, he opened the briefcase he had placed on the table, took out a folder and handed it to her. "If I don't make it past tomorrow, I'd like for you to have this. And please don't say no."

"What is it?"

Before she could open it, he placed a hand over hers to stop, eyes locked together, staring intently, his eyes like liquid fire. "When I denied us, I want you to know it was because I had no choice. The scandal was going to destroy your career."

"You've told me that before, and I said…"

"Shh…" he silenced her. "I remember what you said. Now you need to listen to me."

She nodded gently.

"When you heard that I had denied us, you were hurt. You said that I chose Dahlia again; that I chose my position at Connor Corp over you, and it hurt me that you would actually think that of me. And then you told me to choose you or else we'd be over."

"Ray, I only said that…"

"Shh…" he silenced her again. "If I make it past tomorrow…'

If he made it past tomorrow! The way he kept saying that was beginning to unnerve her. But she tried to listen.

"….I want to tell the world about us, but it might ruin your career. You have paraded yourself as a marriage fixer, and it would not go well with the crowd if you marry your client's husband."

Marry. Did he just say marry? This man was planning to marry her! She smiled on the inside.

"So I'm going to ask you to change professions."

The smile and the happiness on her inside faded away. She jerked her hands away from him. A sick feeling crawled through her belly. "Is that what this is about? You want me to change professions? Just like that..."

"Listen to me. You're getting me wrong."

"Ray!"

"I don't mean leave your job totally. I mean leave this for something more, something wider in range, something greater than what you have now."

The sick feeling crawled away as hope grew in its place. "And what is that?"

He let out a deep breath and regrouped. "Mara, do you trust me?"

She didn't know what to say, so she nodded.

"Then I'm asking you to leave this marriage-fixing thing and become a private investigator."

Did she hear him correctly? A private investigator? What... what...

"Mara, you might have gone into family law, but that was a mistake," he explained. "You like solving puzzles, and saving marriages was just a branch that grew out of your love for solving puzzles. You know what marriage counselors do, right?"

Tamara didn't know what marriage counselors had to do with the conversation at hand, but she answered anyway. "They fix marriages."

"By counseling their clients and making them see the good reasons they loved each other in the first place and, why they should stay married. But you don't do that."

"I investigate their lives, find out their secrets, go to the roots and find out exactly what the problem is. I don't ask them for the problem because I believe they'd lie. I investigate it and connect the dots. I then think of how to use that truth to save their marriage."

He gave her a questioning look. "See? You love solving puzzles."

"Yes," she replied. She didn't need Raymond to tell her this. She had known this about herself for a long time.

Raymond seemed to be holding his breath. "So are you going to become a private investigator?" he asked, his chest vibrating with anticipation and emotion.

Her lips curved into a small smile, and she saw relief wash over his face.

"Yes. Yes. I'll be a private investigator."

It sounded to her like she was saying *Yes, yes, I'll marry you.* Because, in reality, it seemed that was the deal he was offering. *If you marry me, it might ruin your career, so please marry me and lose this career for a bigger one. He said he'd find a way for us to be together. Maybe this is it,* she thought.

"And that's why I decided to buy you that," he said proudly, pointing to the folder in her hands.

She glanced skeptically at him. "What is this?"

He gestured for her to go ahead and open it.

When she did, she read through it for a while.

She was thunderstruck.

Her eyes came, slowly and boldly to his as she gave him a disapproving scowl. "No, Ray, this is too much."

He didn't respond.

So she continued, "This building is worth millions." She shook her head. "No. I can't take it."

Holding her upper arm, he stared intently into her eyes. "You're worth more than this."

His touch sent vibrations through her veins. If he kept touching her like that, he would probably win this argument.

She jerked his hands off her. "Still, I can't take it…"

"Look at me, Mara." Her eyes came gently to his, and she could see that he was serious. He had that kind of frustrated look that said he was in no mood to argue. "If we're going to spend the rest of our lives together, you have to start getting used to do this. This is me showing you how much I love you. This is me showing you that there is nothing too much to give to you. I can give you the whole of Connor Corp as long as it makes you happy. God knows I can."

"But Ray…"

He placed a finger on her lips. "Say nothing," and then he pulled her in into his arms and held her for only God knows how long.

"How am I ever going to repay you?" she softly asked.

"Let me love you. That's how you can repay me." His voice was slightly above a whisper. "And let me hold you like this."

He held her for another long second, until she released herself from his hold. Still staring at him, she pulled his face down and pressed her lips on his, kissing him deeply. It was intoxicating, with a fierce rush of long-denied passion. She leaned against his hard body, so close she could feel the evidence of his arousal.

But then he broke the kiss and held her by the shoulder, his eyes never leaving those charming, dark amber eyes of hers. "Don't do this because you feel indebted to me."

"I've missed you, Ray."

That was the only encouragement he needed. He grabbed her and took her mouth in his, kissing her with the strength of a man going after what he wanted.

Their tongues danced as Tamara used her free arm, the one that wasn't desperately clinging to him, to clear the desk of its clutter and make room for more important activities.

The door had been slammed shut, and the blinds closed. She smiled into the kiss, out of pure anticipation, finally receiving something she had been waiting for far too long for.

She pulled him on top of her, roughly unbuckling his belt as she did so, tossing it to the side where his jacket and her panties also lay. Her laptop was no longer on the table, probably laying broken on the floor somewhere, an acceptable loss.

Every touch was white-hot, and made her want to scream. Oh, how she had missed this. She could feel him pulling back, beginning his game of teasing her, making her want him until she melted into his embrace.

Today, Tamara was not in the mood for that.

Instead, she turned him on his back, forcing him onto the desk. She pulled the black denim downwards, discarding it somewhere she didn't have to look at it. Her arm hurt a little, but she didn't wince. The adrenaline pumping through her veins was better than any pain killer.

She felt a hunger like never before — something that needed to be satisfied immediately.

She pounced atop him, grinding her hips in a way that would drive any man to the brink of ecstasy. The deep groans that fell from his lips proved that. She slowly unbuttoned her blouse, the frilly green material falling to the floor, followed immediately by her black brassiere.

Raymond was not used to this treatment. He was used to dictating the situation, being in control. Here, though, Tamara had taken the reigns, and for some reason, he found himself grinning like a madman.

Her actions were rough and quick, lustful and desiring. She could feel him growing against her, which made her lean her head back and shriek. She hiked her black pencil skirt up and guided him into her.

He let out a surprised gasp as she did, and then smiled ruefully, biting her lip and releasing a moan. She bucked her hips against him, forcing him into submission.

Her hand found its way to his chest, using it as a solid surface to continue riding. Having him inside her was forcing her to lose her grip on reality. She moved as quickly as she could, wanting it more and more, knowing that every second he wasn't in her was a second wasted. Every time he filled her, static rippled through her skin, causing her to whine uncontrollably.

She felt him release inside her with a near scream, and she could no longer hold it. Her body spasmed with a feeling no mere human was meant to have. She screamed in ecstasy.

Tamara collapsed in a sweaty heap over him, still feeling the heat of his skin against hers. He wheezed, breathless and surprised, as she smiled at him, pressing her lips to his once again, letting the waves of pleasure subside into simple comfort.

FOURTEEN

"Is this goodbye?" Raymond asked as he buttoned his shirt.

"No, I'm going to make sure it's not."

He pulled her in and placed a wet, soft kiss on her lips. "I believe you." He moved to kiss her again with the kind of passion that Tamara understood so well.

Still in his arms, she pulled her lips away from his. "You should go. I have work."

"You do not dismiss me."

Wrapping her arms around his neck, she leaned closer and placed a small kiss on his lips. "I know, but you know I have work. And I need some privacy."

His hands slipped under her top and he cupped one breast with his palm. "I don't want to go."

Her gaze moved over him, taking in his broad, muscular shoulders as her hands moved over it.

"That's not making me want to leave," he muttered, kissing the side of her neck.

"Ray!!!" she growled.

"Okay," he said, placing one long kiss on her lips before walking out.

A few seconds after he left, Tamara was still standing there, smiling to herself. The last few minutes kept replaying in her head, and her body resurrected the passion of the moment. Silently, she told her libido to shut up.

Falling to her knees, she began to pick up the documents that had fallen from the table. She sat in her armchair and decided to start with the statement of account.

Tamara wanted to know everybody on Dahlia's payroll. It might help her solve another puzzle and save Ray's life at the same time.

As she studied the statement, everything seemed normal. A couple of purchases at Once Upon a Baby and The Children's Place. Everything seemed normal. Dahlia was just a mother that opened a separate bank account to deal with the affairs of her baby.

She concluded that the bank statement was of no use, but she had to keep reading it. Maybe she was missing something. And as she flipped to the next page, what she saw almost took her breath away.

She was thunderstruck.

$100,000 wired to a Dr. Morgan.

She couldn't continue reading.

How did she miss it? She should have known. She flipped through her mental files and remembered Raymond telling her that Dr. Morgan looked familiar. Had they met before? She needed answers.

Quickly, she packed the rest of the documents into her purse and hurried out of the office.

****

"Start talking!"

Tamara roared as she flung open the door and threw the documents on the table before him.

Dr. Morgan's brow wrinkled in a confusing frown. "Tamara, what's the problem?"

Staring intently into his eyes, she pointed to the document on the table. "$100,000 was secretly wired into your account. So, start talking — now!"

Dr. Morgan flicked through the document, his face turning pale as if he had just seen a ghost. For the next few seconds, he was tongue-tied and couldn't look Tamara in the face. When he finally did, he scowled and swallowed hard. "I don't know what you're talking about."

His denial filled Tamara with so much rage that she wanted to explode in anger. Reflexively, her palm became a fist and hit the table. "I have a lab result that proves that Raymond Connor tested positive for arsenic poisoning. I also have a confession from Dahlia where she admitted to feeding her husband with arsenic. Given that Raymond is still alive, I think I have enough evidence to build an attempted murder case. But if he dies, if he dies tomorrow night as threatened, it's going to break me, and I'm going to have nothing left in this world. That means I get to go after his killers with everything I have, with great, pointy vengeance because I've got nothing to lose anymore. I wouldn't stop till I get the death sentence for Dahlia. And her accomplice, you, Dr. Morgan — your family will weep for you when they see what I will do to you. I will kill you slowly, destroy everything you love. I will make sure you don't get to practice medicine anymore. I will use all the evidence against you, falsify it if I have to, and I won't stop until you get a life sentence. And you know I can do it. So do you still not know what I'm talking about?"

Dr. Morgan shuddered and let the threat sink in. He knew Tamara what Tamara was capable of. She could do the unspeakable when pushed to the wall. He let out a heavy sigh. "I needed the money at the time, but not a day passes by that what I did doesn't weigh on my conscience."

Tamara folded her arms, listening intently to him.

"Raymond was sick. His doctors had done several tests to find out what was wrong with him, but they found nothing. At that point, they thought it might be toxins, so they invited me in as a consultant."

He paused and looked away, unable to look at Tamara.

She unfolded her arms, leaned her hands on the table and let her gaze follow his. "Well, what happened?"

"A man contacted me. It was a man. It wasn't Dahlia like you thought. I don't know his name. Never met him, but it was a man."

A man? If it wasn't Dahlia, why was he paid with an account opened in the name of her baby, the same account that Dahlia used to pay Sherry? Someone else had access to that account. Who else could have access to that kind of account? Only the child's parents. Tamara needed answers, but she kept listening to Dr. Morgan.

"The man said he would pay me $100,000, and all I had to do was convince the doctors that it wasn't a toxin. I'm a toxicologist, so it was easy for me to get the job done. I manipulated the test results and convinced the other doctors."

Tamara let out a deep breath and sank into the armchair opposite of him.

"But I gave him something," he quickly added. "I couldn't let the man die just like that. I prescribed a med that will suppress the symptoms and give him the strength to live his daily life." His voice became gentler. "You don't know how happy I was when you brought him back to me. I was even happier when he didn't recognize me. It was as if God gave me another chance to correct my mistake. And I've been doing just that. Raymond is responding well to treatment, and he's going to be alright."

Tamara lowered her head as if deep in thought, her brow drawn together as she bit her lower lip.

"Tamara?" Dr. Morgan asked.

Raising her head, she looked at him.

"What are you going to do… about me?"

She grabbed the documents and folded them back into her purse. "I don't know yet."

"I'm sorry. I really am. I needed the money at the time and…"

Nothing was making sense. Her head was spinning. She was trying hard to see what she was missing. She needed to be alone and think about everything all over again from the start.

Quickly, she lifted her purse and began to walk out of Dr. Morgan's office.

Dr. Morgan stood from his chair, trying to stop her. "Tamara!"

She halted.

"There's something you must know." He hesitated for a second. "Raymond said he didn't usually eat a lot at home. Judging from the amount of arsenic in him, there must be another source."

Very slowly, Tamara turned back to look at him, her eyes wide. "What?"

"I'm guessing it's not only Dahlia. Someone else is feeding him with arsenic."

Everything was beginning to make sense. Tamara flipped through her mental files, Raymond's words repeating themselves in her mind. *Someone makes my coffee in the office every day — you don't think that person could be feeding me with arsenic?* And then Joe's words flashed through her mind.

Or just go ahead and call Anita, his assistant. She knows more about his whereabouts than I do.

Her lips curled into a sly smile. Tamara had to admit whoever was the brains behind all of this was very smart. He placed a wife in Raymond's life to kill him slowly at home, a personal assistant to slowly kill at the office, and a doctor to prevent his ailment from getting treated. He was damned smart! But who knew how many more people around Raymond had been corrupted?

"Oh. My. Gosh," Tamara said slowly. "The wedding anniversary party!"

Very quickly, she pulled her cellphone from her purse and placed a call to Raymond. "Ray!" she said as soon as he picked up the call, her heart heaving heavily. "Whatever you do, do not eat anything at the party tomorrow."

"I told you to stop digging. Stop!"

"Do not eat anything at the party!" she repeated. "And I have a quick question for you. The trip you took to Dallas—was Joe Connor on that trip with you?"

"Yes. Why?"

"Was he at the bar with you when you met Dahlia?"

"No. He lodged at another hotel."

"Okay, thanks. Now, do not eat anything at the party!"

Before he could respond, she hung up.

"These people, they're not going to stop until they kill him," Dr. Morgan said.

Tamara ignored him and walked out of his office. She wasn't going to stop until he was safe.

****

It was early the next morning when Tamara drove to Bishop Shepherd's residence. Throughout the night, she couldn't sleep. All she kept thinking about was how to actually pull this off. She had been able to put things together, and everything made sense now. She even thought she knew who wanted Raymond dead. If she was right, then she needed more hands to actually pull off her plan.

As she slammed her feet on the brakes and parked in front of Bishop Shepherd's residence, she hated the fact that she had to bring him into this, but she didn't have any choice. She needed help, and she'd do whatever it took. Yes, whatever it took.

She pressed the doorbell and waited patiently. Like she expected, Linda was really happy to see her. Tamara had come to her rescue at a time when she thought there was no hope. She had saved her marriage.

"Tamara, nice to see you again," Linda said with a big smile as she gave Tamara a warm hug.

"Nice to see you, too," Tamara replied.

The smile quickly disappeared from Linda's face. "We heard about it on the news. I'm so sorry."

Tamara stared on for a while, confused, and then it hit her. Linda was referring to the news about her affair with Raymond, the one that almost ruined her career.

"Oh! Everything is okay now. I got through it, and the firm is surviving."

"Thank God!" she said with a smile

"I'm here to see the Bishop. Is he in?"

"Yes, he is." She held open the door and stepped to the side. "Please, come in. And don't mind my attitude. I was so excited to see you, I forgot to invite you in."

Tamara smiled, walked in and sat on the couch.

"What would you like to drink?"

"Coffee. No sugar, no cream."

"How you take your coffee says a lot about you," Linda said as she walked into the kitchen.

"And what does it say about me?"

"Nothing that you don't already know," she replied.

Before Linda returned with the coffee, Bishop came into the living room, arms open wide. "Tamara, it's nice to see you again."

Tamara stood up and gave him a slight hug with a bright smile. "Nice to see you, too."

Bishop sat on the couch next to her. "You don't want anything to eat?"

"Linda is making me coffee."

At that moment, Linda came back with the coffee.

Tamara took the coffee from her, took a sip and placed the cup on the table. "So, how are you doing?" she asked.

They talked and talked, joked and laughed together. They had a lot of catching up to do.

After several minutes of chatting, Tamara went straight to business. "Bishop, I need your help."

FIFTEEN

The Grand Chesapeake Ballroom at the Bright Star Hotel was perfumed with riches and sophistication. It glittered with elaborate crystal chandeliers and the precious jewels worn by smartly dressed, elegant women. It was no doubt a gathering only for the elite. Whether Raymond Connor liked it or not, this was normal for him. Ever since the news broke that he was the son of billionaire James Connor and that he was in charge of the Connor wealth, his life had changed. Suddenly, everybody saw him as someone they had to impress, or get in his good graces so they could have a bit of his money, power, and prestige. They wanted a glimpse of the influential life of being a Connor. No matter how much Raymond hated it, he could only accept and embrace it.

Raymond managed a bright smile as he extended a hand to a guest. In a split second, a few others joined in and formed a small circle around him as they engaged in light chat. As usual, they were all playing a part and giving their fake smiles as they spoke about whatever unimportant things guests spoke about.

As they stood in the small gathering, Dahlia held his hand tightly, making sure not to let go of him for a microsecond. Raymond reflexively looked at her. One year had crawled by, slowly dragging the life out of him. Literally. He could swear it had been an eternity since he had been forced into a life with this woman. He thought the 'till death' clause would have been closer to fruition by now. Because on this night, as they all gathered to celebrate their one-year wedding anniversary, Raymond knew it was the celebration of his death. This very night, he was going to take his last breath, and he knew it.

Music began and Dahlia stood pressed against him, slowly swaying to the beat of the music, her dark cocktail dress shimmering in the artificial light. He smiled gently at her, and she returned it, her lips breaking to reveal a perfect, white crescent. She was beautiful without a doubt. However, Raymond was not the kind of man who could love on beauty alone. He'd be lying if he said he hadn't tried. He had tried, for the sake of their son.

He kissed her tenderly, squeezing her hands as he did so— all of it an act. He suppressed a single sigh as, once again, the kiss did not spark anything in his heart. There was no desire or love for her.

A cool, titillating air coursed through him, causing him to look towards the door of the dimmed ballroom. His breath caught for an instant. No matter what was happening around him, he couldn't take his eyes away from that door because there stood Tamara Price, the woman who eased his suffering and made him forget the pain of his marriage as one forgets the name of a stranger never to be seen again. The woman with whom he shared a connection so strong that he was continually drawn to her in a way he had never experienced before. The woman with whom he shared a love so deep, strong and complex, that he doubted if he had ever truly loved anyone before her. And after her, there could be no one else. He'd never want or love any other woman like he loved her.

Tamara stood, her dress a simple, deep scarlet that shone brightly against her perfect dark skin, framing her hourglass shape with an effortless grace, her jacket already taken by some star-struck fool. The dark tresses of her hair fell in perfect curls around her face, accentuating her high cheekbones and bringing out the light brown in her eyes. Her lips parted as she saw him, and she smiled with an elegance that demanded his attention. And she got his attention because he felt his manhood spring to attention.

Dahlia's voice broke through his reverie.

"I invited her," she whispered.

She must have noticed him staring at Tamara. His gaze left Tamara for a split second and went to Dahlia. "You invited Mara?"

She nodded, almost sadly. "You miss her, and I thought that seeing her would make you happy. I'd do anything for you, Raymond."

Raymond tried to concentrate on his supposed wife of a year, but only became more disappointed in everything about her. She was flawed and imperfect, like every woman.   Every woman except Tamara — the woman he wanted.

Finally, after what seemed like years, the song slowed down and it was time to change partners. He was released from Dahlia's grip and by some miracle, Tamara was his next partner.

The moment her hands slid into his, he felt his heart skip a beat. The fake smile that had been plastered on his face became all too real.

Once again she smiled that graceful smile, something so beautiful it almost took his breath away.

"Congratulations on your one-year anniversary, Mr. Connor," she said quietly, her beautiful voice matching the sparks in her eyes.

"Mr. Connor?" He shook his head slowly. "That is not sexy. Is Mr. Connor a boring librarian?"

"Maybe I should call you Mr. Bossy Billionaire. That would be sexy, right?"

His hands went to her waist and jolted her closer to him. "You know that's not what I mean."

Their bodies were so close that he could swear he felt the soft touch of her boobs. It

was enough to start a fire down there, and he pressed her closely to himself, his eyes watching her beautiful face and the rising and falling of her chest. He couldn't be more certain that she felt it, too. She fully felt the emotions that had been exploding since the instant they held each other for this dance.

"People are watching," she said as they waddled slowly together, looking into each other's eyes.

"Watching what?" he asked.

"Your eyes. They are naked with emotion. And you're looking so lovingly into my eyes, holding me so close, I can feel your breath on my face. People are watching."

"They can watch if they want to. I don't care."

"Well, for a guy who wouldn't choose me and would rather throw a large anniversary party for his wife, it's a surprise that you don't care that people are watching."

Raymond didn't say anything, and he didn't stop looking at her. His hot gaze was beginning to stir up the passions that lived in both of their veins.

"Would you stop?" Tamara said in whispers as she tried to harden her voice.

He gave his arrogant I-don't-give-a-damn smile. "Stop what?"

"This. People are going to talk. You're going to create another scandal."

"Mara!" he whispered.

"You like being in the news, right? Scandal kind of agrees with you."

"After yesterday, do you really think I don't love you enough to choose you?"

"Yes," she replied, trying not to meet his gaze.

"Yesterday, I was practically asking you to marry me. You can read between the lines, can't you?"

"I didn't hear you ask me that yesterday."

"Really? What does it mean when I said if you marry me, you will lose your career, so please be with me and lose your career?"

"Maybe I agree with you that you asked me into your life yesterday. But then today, you're throwing a lavish party for your anniversary. It's contradictory. It's not love."

"So now you doubt that I love you?" She didn't respond. He breathed hard and regrouped. "I tell you I love you every day. I sing it to your ears. I'll do anything for you. I'll give my life for you. And you still think I don't love you? I should be the one thinking you don't love me because you hardly say it."

"Still, I think you can't choose me. You're not capable of it. You don't have what it takes to face the consequences. There's too much at stake if…"

Her words were interrupted as the music stopped and Raymond let go of her. Grabbing a cup of champagne from a nearby waiter, Raymond gulped down the drink. He gave the same fate to one more cup, and then walked confidently to the podium, the guests applauding him all the way.

"Thank you," he said as the applause slowly came to a stop. Before he could say more, he felt a mild dryness in his mouth. He felt dehydrated, as if he needed more liquid. Feeling dehydrated wasn't such a big deal, so he ignored the feeling.

"Ladies and gentlemen," he began, "thank you all for coming here today and for sharing this special day with us. But before I give my very long vote-of-thanks speech, I have a confession to make." Again, he felt an intense cramp in his stomach. A sharp tightening in his chest brought him to a halt. He felt breathing becoming more difficult. What the heck was going on?

His gaze went briefly to the waiter who served him his drink. The waiter was gone. Lord help him! He just unknowingly took the last dose of arsenic.

Death was imminent, but he had to make this confession. After everything they'd been through, Tamara deserved it. The sharp pain in his chest was becoming unbearable, and as he tried to hold it in, the tears that had gathered in his eyes glittered in the artificial light.

Eyes fixed on Tamara, he began, "I'm in love with a woman who is not my wife." His vision became blurry, and he tried to summon the last of his strength. "That incredible woman is Tamara Price."

The ballroom erupted into a mass of noise and confusion. The few pressmen in the room rushed toward him to get more information. Feeling as if his legs couldn't hold him up any longer, he crouched on one knee. He felt a little constricted in his throat and coughed to clear it. Blood gushed out in pulsing ripples.

People were taken aback and stood frozen. Tamara rushed through the crowd and climbed to the podium. Kneeling at his side with her face awash with tears, she held him. "Ray! Ray! Stay with me! Ray!"

Raymond clutched his chest as he struggled and gasped for breath. After so much struggling, he gave up.

Tamara yelled, "Call 911!"

****

In a split second, an ambulance siren blasted out at full volume. While Raymond was moved into the ambulance, Tamara attempted to get in the ambulance.

Dahlia's eyes burned with rage. "No, you can't!" she yelled.

"I have to!" Tamara replied.

"Only family is needed here."

"You don't understand, Dahlia. I have to be there with him."

There was no way she was going to leave Raymond alone in the hands of two traitors. Who knows what they would do to him once they were in the ambulance with him.

Joe Connor patted Tamara's shoulder. "Tamara, Dahlia is right. You can't get in the ambulance with us." His voice was gentle. "We want only family here."

"I'll go with him," said a deep, baritone voice.

Tamara turned to see who it was. "Bishop Shepherd! You came?"

He walked closer and gave her a light hug. "I owed you one," he whispered.

"Thanks, Bishop," she replied.

He released her from the hug and turned to Joe and Dahlia. "I'm Bishop Shepherd, Raymond's pastor. He might need only family, but he also needs prayers, so I'll ride with him in this ambulance."

Joe gave a slight nod, and Tamara's lips curved into a slight smile.

This just in: Moments after Connor Corp CEO Raymond Connor confirmed his affair with divorce attorney Tamara Price, he went into cardiac arrest. However, we have unconfirmed reports from hospital staff that Raymond Connor collapsed because his food or drink contained arsenic poison. We'll have more on this story as it develops.

SIXTEEN

"I'm afraid I have some bad news," Dr. Morgan said, his voice gentle.

Joe and Dahlia stepped closer, jittery with fear and anticipation.

Tamara stood a few steps away, but not too close because she wasn't family. Just close enough to listen in on the conversation.

"Despite the best efforts of the paramedics, nurses, doctors, and modern technology, I'm sorry, but Mr. Connor passed away. He didn't suffer throughout the resuscitation process."

Tamara didn't think she heard right. Color drained from her face; her jaw slackened as she stared into pure nothingness. She let out a sudden sigh and tried to speak, but nothing came.

She and Raymond had only gotten back together in the past few weeks, but it was... it was... she lacked the words to express how wonderful it had been.

Ever since Raymond came back into her life, all of her thoughts had revolved around him. Every breath had been for him. She had tried to avert this, but she failed. She failed him.

She was frozen to a point that she looked like she wasn't breathing at all. A hand helped her to a chair, but she didn't know who. She could hear the bishop saying they should take heart, and that Raymond had gone to a better place. And then she thought she heard the doctor say that it was okay for everyone to go into the ward one at a time to visit Raymond before they arranged for autopsy.

"Joe! Dahlia! Come with me. Immediately."

The harsh, cold voice jolted Tamara out of the shock. Her eyes went to see who it was. It was Lisa Connor, a woman in the autumn of her life. If Tamara had to guess, she'd say she was in her late fifties. Deep, wrinkled lines that could not be hidden by her many plastic surgeries and large amount of make-up distorted her face, but there was no mistaking her strength in those sea-blue eyes.

If there was one person Tamara was afraid of, it was Lisa. She was smart, intelligent, ruthless, and knew people in the right places. The last time Tamara faced off with this woman, she won because Lisa let her. Lisa made Tamara. She was the reason Tamara could go to any length to get things done. She was the reason Tamara believed that the end justified the means.

It happened way back when James Connor named Raymond Brock as the heir to Connor Corp and the Connor family wealth. Raymond had hired her. She thought it was going to be an easy job. The late James Connor had a will written out, kept safe with his lawyer. Everything seemed easy.

But Lisa was very good at making matters complicated. When the legal battle began, Lisa murdered James Connor's lawyer in cold blood, stole the original copy of the will and destroyed it. And guess what? She got away with it. And even though Tamara knew she killed this lawyer, she had no proof. No evidence. All the evidence she tried to present was thrown out of court on the grounds of being "coincidental." It didn't prove she committed murder.

And since the will had been destroyed, there was also no way to prove that James had named Raymond as his heir.

But Tamara couldn't let her win just like that, so she went to the extreme, against everything she believed in. She falsified a new will, getting the best forgers in the world to fake James Connor's signature, and then presented it as the original will. Lisa knew the will was fake, but she had no way to prove it. She couldn't confess to destroying the original, since her confession would become a motive for the lawyer's murder. Lisa kept her mouth shut.

In the end, they reached a reasonable agreement and the case was closed. Before that, Lisa told her she knew that the will Tamara had presented was fake, but she was going to let it go. And that's only because it seemed that Joe and Raymond were getting along. She realized that Raymond wasn't selfish and was willing to share the wealth with his brothers accordingly.

After that, Tamara hadn't set eyes on Lisa. She tried to look for her, combed the world trying to find her, but it seemed as if she had disappeared from the face of the earth. And now she stood right in front of her again, her face dead cold.

"Joe! Dahlia!" she called again, impatience evident in her voice.

Joe walked to his mother and held her wrists. "Mom, not now. Ray is gone," he said, speaking through the lump in his throat, his eyes turning red like someone trying hard to hold back tears. "So, please, Mom, not now."

Lisa jerked her wrists from his hold and walked closer to Dr. Morgan. Her face was gentle and calm, but her voice was firm. "Thank you, doctor, for your efforts in trying to save my son."

What? She referred to Raymond as her son!

"But right now, we want to grieve quietly. We want to find closure quickly. That's why I'm going to ask you to bypass the medical procedures and stop the autopsy. Myself and the rest of the Connor family thank you very much for your help." She talked with so much confidence that it might take Tamara three lifetimes to actually attain that kind of confidence and style.

Dr. Morgan nodded.

And then she turned very quickly to Joe and Dahlia. "Both of you have to come with me now." She concentrated her gaze on Joe. "Especially you. Very soon, the board of directors is going to find out about Raymond's death, and a lot of them are going to want to sit in his chair. You are not a member of the board and don't have a right to that seat, but if you don't want everything your father and I worked for to go down the drain, you have to come with me right now. Ben Murray is going to help you get your birthright."

Joe tried to man up and glared at his mother, his face red and angry. "This is not the time or place to start talking about business."

"Joe!" She yelled at him to silence.

Tamara decided it was time to speak, so she cleared her throat to make appearance. All eyes went straight to her. She stood and walked closer to Lisa, trying to build up that same confidence within herself. "Actually, Joe wouldn't need anyone's help because Raymond left a will and already decided who should take over for him. According to the rules and agreements set forth in the Connor Corp charter, the present chairman of the board has a right to choose his successor."

Lisa's face was expressionless, showing absolutely no emotion. It rarely did. No anger, no softness, no love, just blank. "I'm done playing hide and seek with you, Tamara Price. Stay out of my family affair this time."

If she was playing it calm, Tamara decided to play it calm, too. "I'm sorry, Mrs. Connor, I'm already involved in this. I am Raymond's attorney," she said calmly. "But since you're eager to get this over with quickly, I'll work at your pace. We'll meet at 8 a.m. tomorrow morning at Raymond's place, and I'll let you know the content of the will. And maybe after that, you'll let me bury Raymond in peace."

Lisa nodded and raised her shoulder in a shrug. "Tomorrow morning it is," she replied and then glanced at Joe. "You're coming with me now!" she said in a tone that refused to be challenged.

Joe didn't respond.

And then she glanced at Dahlia. "And you—are you coming or staying?"

"I'm coming with you," she replied.

Hell, she is, the vicious gold digger.

****

The next morning, Tamara wore a black Calvin Klein dress and black, six-inch heels. She was still mourning. Anyone could easily notice it on her face. She looked worn-out, tired, hurt and angry. She hadn't had time to think things through, and she sure as hell hadn't had time to cry. Not now. She needed to be strong now. She couldn't afford to crash down like that. Lisa Connor had made it obvious that they didn't care about Raymond. All they cared about was the stupid Connor wealth.

She would let them know the content of the will, and then she would request his corpse to bury him with the honor he deserved. After all that was done, she could crash. She could mourn him, stay in bed for days. Cry.

Hot tears filled her eyes. She swayed her head slightly, trying not to shed any tears.

"Not now, Mara. Not now," she said to herself.

She wiped the tears away very quickly. Her head ached badly from trying to hold them back.

When she parked her car in front of Raymond's mansion, she almost went into another nervous crisis. Breathe in. Breathe out. In. Out. In. Out.

You can do this, she told herself and stepped out of the car, holding a folder in her hands. When she walked into the living room, everybody was seated and waiting for her—except Lisa. Dahlia and Joe sat together on a double chair. Anita sat on a single chair. Anita may not have been family, but she was a beneficiary in Raymond's will.

They hardly said two words of greetings to Tamara, except Joe, who asked how she was holding up. She told him she was doing alright and tried to feign a smile before taking a seat.

They waited in silence for Lisa. A few minutes later, Lisa walked in and took a seat next to Anita. "Shall we begin?" she asked.

"Not yet," Tamara replied, concentrating her gaze on the folder. "We're still waiting for someone."

Lisa didn't respond. They waited again in silence.

Tamara smiled to herself. She had crushed Lisa already. Lisa loved to be the one to set things in motion. Her arrival should have set the reading of the will in motion, but Tamara had ruined her powerful entrance. She stole a quick glance at her. Her face showed no emotions, but Tamara could tell she was angry as hell. She could just tell.

A slight knock took all their attention to the door. Dahlia stood up and went to open it.

He came in and said hello. The response was low. Everyone was staring at him, wondering who the hell he was.

"Everyone, meet Detective Lance."

Detective Lance said hello again and sat next to Tamara. Two other cops in uniform stood behind them.

"Why did you bring the police into this?"

Tamara gave a light shrug. "No reason. I just don't trust that y'all wouldn't beat me up after hearing what's in the will."

Lisa scoffed. "Who cares? We're not planning to honor that will anyway."

Her lips curled into a small smile. "Don't be too sure."

"Shall we begin?" she asked again.

"Of course." Tamara opened the folder, cleared her throat and stood. "This session is about his real properties." She glanced at their faces and saw that they showed no interest in that session of the will. "I give my entire interest in the real property which was my residence at the time of my death, together with any insurance on such real property, but subject to any encumbrances on said real property, to my lovely wife, Dahlia Connor. If said devisee fails to survive me, then this gift shall lapse and become part of the residue of my estate."

She glanced at their faces again. "The next session is in regard to the controlling shares of the parent company, Connor Corp."

They all adjusted in their seats. This was where their interest lay.

"The controlling shares will be divided among three..." she paused and raised an eyebrow for emphasis. "The division is as follows: ten percent to Anita."

Surprises covered their faces and a neat smile spread across Anita's face.

"Forty percent to Josh Connor. And the last fifty percent..." Tamara could see their chest rising and falling with anticipation. "...and the last fifty percent to Joe Connor, which makes Joe the new CEO of Connor Corp and the chairman of the board of directors. I nominate Joe to serve as executor of my estate and the sole controller of all the Connor wealth left behind."

Lisa smiled and for the first time since Tamara had known her, real happiness flashed in her eyes.

"I have intentionally omitted making provision for my heir, Richard Connor. I generally and specifically disinherit Richard Connor because he is not my son and therefore not a Connor, and therefore has no right to any of the Connor wealth."

"BULLSHIT!!!!!!!!" Dahlia yelled.

Shit just got real. Tamara stifled a grin.

Dahlia stood up, anger flaring in her eyes, her body hot as if someone was boiling her blood. "This is all bullshit! My son is a Connor!"

"With all due respect, Dahlia, I have a copy of the results of the DNA test performed on your son by late Mr. Connor," Tamara said, her voice even.

Dahlia shot her a glare. "I don't give a fuck about any damn DNA test. My son is a Connor."

"Dahlia," Lisa called softly, "we'll do something about you and your son, but please allow us to make preparations to accept the terms of this will." Her voice remained pleasant, the hint of a smile still plastered on her face.

"Nobody is accepting this will! That cheating son of a bitch left nothing for my son! Oh, I'm glad he's dead."

"Dahlia!" Joe yelled. He hadn't said anything since the reading of the will. His face didn't even reflect if he was happy with everything he got. "Stop this right now. At least you got something."

Dahlia scowled. "I got this damn house!"

"That is something," he replied. "We will do something about Richard, but first we must honor my brother's wishes by accepting this will."

"How dare you talk about accepting this will? How dare you? Richard is your son, dammit!"

There. She said it.

"What?" Joe asked, pulling his brow together in confusion.

"My gosh! This family is sick," Dahlia said. "After everything y'all made me do, all I get is a stupid house and my son disinherited?"

"What did they make you do?" Tamara asked, her voice not accusing, just even and soft.

Dahlia glanced at Tamara and hot tears gathered at the corner of her eyes, and she went calm. "Raymond was a good person," she began, tears in her voice. "He is one of the most beautiful souls that ever lived on this earth. He was capable of loving. Especially you, Tamara." She cast a quick glance at her. "But these people…"

"Dahlia!" Lisa's voice was hard. Her fiery blue eyes glared as she cast a look at the detective, and then back to Dahlia. She gritted her teeth. "Stop talking!"

As if Dahlia had just noticed the police, she sat back down on the couch, quiet.

"Well, if you will not let her talk, I will." Tamara said and began to pace. "When Raymond Connor inherited Connor Corp, the rest of the Connors weren't happy about it. Dahlia was Joe's girlfriend, and she knew she was carrying Joe's baby. At first, I thought Dahlia was acting alone—that she was selfish and had intentionally gone after Raymond, slept with him and lied about carrying his baby just so she could get the brother who controlled the wealth, but I was wrong." She stopped pacing and stood right in front of Joe, staring straight into his eyes. "Joe Connor, you orchestrated the conspiracy to kill your brother!"

"What!"

"Dahlia was your girlfriend, but you used her to get to Raymond. You conspired with Anita, Raymond's personal assistant. Anita told you Raymond would be in Dallas, and you sent Dahlia after him. Raymond fell for it and slept with Dahlia. But Dahlia couldn't work her charms right, because, to your surprise, Raymond didn't try to continue the affair with Dahlia. And when Dahlia told you that she was carrying your baby, you saw an opportunity. You used Anita again. She told you Raymond was on a trip to Paris, and you sent Dahlia after him again. And you had Dahlia lie to him that what they did had become a baby. Raymond tried to do the right thing so he married Dahlia.

"When Dahlia got married to Raymond, you were happy because you had everything in place. You placed a wife in his life and a personal assistant. These two were supposed to get the job done for you. You supplied them a lot of arsenic to feed to Raymond. Dahlia fed him arsenic at home. Anita fed him arsenic at the office. And going by the doctor's report, Raymond died of chronic arsenic poisoning."

She lowered herself and looked straight into Joe's eyes with the kind of expression that said she was certain of what she was talking about. "I put it to you, Joe Connor, that you murdered your brother so that you could take over his position at Connor Corp, but the one thing you didn't know was that he loved you so much that he had already planned to give it to you."

The sound of a clap caught Tamara's attention. She glanced around to see who it was clapping. Lisa. It was Lisa.

She stopped clapping and smiled genuinely at Tamara. "Nice assumptions, but your assumptions aren't evidence. You've got no evidence, no proof and no case."

Tamara straightened her back. "Of course I have evidence. I have Dahlia's confession, Richard Connor is an evidence of Joe and Dahlia's relationship, I have a motive for why Joe would want Raymond dead, and I have a document that links Joe to this crime."

Joe swallowed hard. "I did not kill my brother. I loved Raymond."

"Shut up, Joe," Lisa said. "Let me handle it." Not willing to give Tamara the advantage of height, she stood up to meet her and stepped closer, her icy blue eyes cutting through Tamara. "You have no evidence. You're bluffing."

"Really? Am I?" She went for her purse, picked up her cellphone and played Dahlia's confession for everybody to hear.

You threatened to destroy the two things I loved most — Raymond and my job. My career almost got destroyed when you broke that news, and now Raymond has tested positive for arsenic poisoning. You did it, I'm sure.

Of course I did it.

She pressed the stop button and smiled. "You still think I'm bluffing?" she asked.

Lisa didn't respond.

"And I have the statement of the secret account owned by Dahlia and Joe in the name of their son, Richard Connor. The statement shows all their transaction."

"What account are you talking about?" Joe asked. "I swear to God, I did not kill my brother."

Lisa stared hard at Tamara, her eyes laced with tears. "Joe didn't do it. He didn't kill Raymond. Don't bring my son into this. He didn't do it."

It was the first time Tamara ever saw Lisa show any kind of emotion. She cared about her son, after all. "How can you be so sure he didn't do it?"

"Because... because..." she stuttered. "Because... I... d... dammit! Because I just know. I know my son, and he would never do this"

"That's not enough," she said and glanced at detective Lance. "Detective, please, do your job."

The uniformed officers cuffed Dahlia and Anita, while Detective Lance went for Joe, cuffing his hands behind his back. "You're under arrest for the attempted murder of Raymond Connor."

"Attempted murder?" they asked, surprise evident in their faces.

Tamara smiled. "Yes, attempted murder. Raymond is still very much alive."

"You have the right to an attorney," Detective Lance continued. "And you have the right to remain silent. Whatever you say can and will be used against you in a court of law."

Tamara gave Lisa a proud smile. "I won. Again."

"You've won nothing, my little girl," she said, her voice as condescending as it had ever been, crushing every pride in Tamara. "This is just the beginning."

Tamara managed to retain the smile on her face. "Arrogant till the end, huh?"

SEVENTEEN

Raymond had awakened to find a flashlight shining into his eyes and two weak eyes staring into his.

"He's awake," Dr. Morgan said.

"Where am I?" were the first words out of Raymond's mouth. Sitting up, he glanced around and recognized many faces—Dr. Morgan, and then Drake and Sherry and Megan.

"You're at the hospital," Dr. Morgan replied, his voice gentle. "You passed out at the wedding anniversary party last night."

Everything came rushing back to him. The dance with Mara. Mara provoked him, he drank two cups of champagne, went to the podium to make an announcement and then collapsed. "I didn't die?" he asked.

"You didn't."

"How? I thought my drink was laced with arsenic."

"No, it wasn't." Drake said, taking a few steps closer to the bed. "It was all planned by Tamara. We only did that to make your family believe that you were dead so we could expose the people behind the poisoning."

What? Mara planned this whole thing without letting him know. What had she done? She just ruined everything.

"Exposed?" he asked. "Does that mean involving the police?"

"Yes," Drake replied.

The Lord help him! Mara had just brought hell down on everybody. Glancing around, he saw his shirt neatly hanged. He rose from the bed and grabbed his shirt.

"You need rest," Dr. Morgan said.

"I feel fine. What I need is to get out of here right now before things get out of hand."

He finished buttoning his shirt and went for the door. Drake ran after him, catching up with him and putting himself in front of him. "You can't leave."

Raymond was taken aback. He arched a brow. "Are you holding me hostage?"

"If you want to see it that way, then yes, we are. But Tamara asked that you remain here until she gets back—until she finishes dealing with your family and exposes every single one of them for what they really are. So, what I'm saying is, you can't leave."

Walking past Drake, he tried to force the door open. Try as he might, the door didn't open. It was locked. He walked back, grimacing in pain. "You don't get it. I have to be out of here. Now!"

"I'm sorry, but you can't leave," Drake replied.

He glanced at Sherry, his eyes pleading for her to reason with him. "Sherry?"

"I'm sorry, Mr. Connor, Tamara made her orders clear," Sherry replied.

He let out a deep breath of frustration.

A few minutes later, the door opened and Tamara stepped in. Her face was radiant and a big smile sat on her face. She walked proudly over to Raymond. "It's done," she said.

"What's done?"

"Your family assumed that you were dead. And then I made up a fake will, read it to them and it caused a commotion. In the heat of the moment, the truth came out. Richard isn't your son — he's Joe's. Joe wanted you dead. I presented Dahlia's confession and all the evidence to the police. Joe, Dahlia and Anita are in police custody as we speak. It's done. The battle is over."

Raymond frowned. "What did you do?" he yelled. His voice was harsher and louder than he had intended, but that didn't matter.

Tamara was taken aback by his outburst. Confusion ran over her face. Before she could say anything, her phone rang. She looked over at the phone. "I have to take this," she said. And then she pressed the green button. "Detective Lance?"

"What?!" she screamed. She stood frozen in shock as tears gathered in the corners of her eyes. "How… how… did it happen?"

Slowly, her hand lowered itself. Everyone stared at her, wondering what was going on.

"Dahlia is dead!"

Raymond covered his face with both of his palms. When he removed them, he closed his eyes and grimaced in emotional pain.

"Dahlia was supposed to be in the police custody. How did this happen?"

Raymond shot her a glare. "You're still asking how it happened?"

Tamara was quiet. She had never seen Raymond this angry, this vicious. His face was scary. Anger flashed in his eyes, his voice was icy like a winter night.

"You let this happen!" he yelled.

"Lisa did this!" she replied.

"She did it because you crossed her; because you were going to send her son to jail. I told you how ruthless she can be. I told you she had eyes everywhere. She killed Dahlia to make sure she doesn't confess and mention names. There's no case! You let this happen, Tamara!" All affection was lost in his voice, and for the first time ever, he said her full name.

Tamara shivered. "I was only trying to help."

"I told you to stay out of this. I warned you not to get the police involved, but you're so goddamn stubborn. You don't listen. You planned everything on your own. You didn't even try to run it by me. You didn't think I had a say in the matter. You didn't ask for my opinion because it didn't matter. You are always right. Only your opinion matters."

"Raymond, stop! I was trying to get justice for you."

"No! If you believed in justice, why didn't you hand Dr. Morgan over to the police? He was an accomplice. You gave him another chance. You think you have the right to play God and decide who should get punished and who should get a second chance."

"Ray!"

"I love you so much, Mara. Because I love you and will do anything for you, you take that to be weakness on my part."

"I was trying to help!"

"No! That wasn't you trying to help. That was you making all the decisions. That was you controlling me. You shut me out of everything. It was supposed to be me and you working things out, getting through things together. But instead it was you and your team making decisions about my life. And now you have sent an innocent man to jail and brought the wrath of the devil herself down on us all. Lisa won't stop until everything is destroyed."

"You keep saying Joe is innocent. He isn't. He was trying to kill you."

"No! No, he wasn't."

"I'm sure."

"No, you only saw and believed what I wanted you to believe."

"What are you trying to say?"

He was quiet for a while, considering whether to let Mara know the truth, the secret he had kept from her just to protect her. He let out a deep breath, and then tried to explain everything that was hidden. When he inherited Connor Corp, Lisa threatened him before going underground. She said it wasn't over. For months, Raymond couldn't sleep with both eyes closed. And when he married Dahlia and brought her home, Joe warned him. He told him that Dahlia was up to no good; that Dahlia used to be his girlfriend, and if she suddenly came to Raymond, she was coming for the Connor wealth. And then he realized something. He ordered a DNA test and learned Richard wasn't his. But he also knew there was no way Dahlia could have known about his connection to Connor Corp unless someone told her. And that someone was Lisa. He stayed married to Dahlia, trying to see if he could use Dahlia to find Lisa. He tried. Hired the best p.i.'s, but they couldn't find her. She didn't want to be found. And when he became sick and the doctors couldn't diagnose his ailment, he suspected Lisa had something to do with it. Again and again, he tried to find Lisa to reason with her, to come to some kind of agreements, but he still couldn't find Lisa.

Things took a different turn when Tamara was able to confirm his ailment as arsenic poisoning. More than ever, he was certain that Lisa was responsible. He had it reinvestigated. And that was how he knew about Dr. Morgan and Anita working with Lisa. He took the treatment, kept cool and decided to turn the situation to his advantage. He gave Tamara the go ahead to work on the case, but not without influencing her investigations.

"What do you mean by influencing my investigation?"

"That Richard Connor account, it was me. I made it up so that it would lead you to Joe."

"But why?"

"Why? Because I wanted you to think it's Joe. I wanted you to come to me with the information that Joe was trying to kill me, and then I was going to make a big deal out of it. Throw Joe out of Connor Corp just so Lisa would come out of her hiding to rescue him. And then I could reason with her, give her Connor Corp if that's what it will take for me to be happy and safe and to give you the happy ending you deserve—a life with me, without any drama."

"But why me? You could have hired a p.i. to do the investigation. Why me?"

"Because you and Lisa have history together."

She let out a deep breath, shaking her head in disbelief. "I don't believe you. You're trying to cover up for Joe. I mean, Dr. Morgan admitted to receiving payment through that Richard Connor account."

"No, he didn't. He admitted to receiving payment, but not through that account. Lisa is smart. She wouldn't be so stupid that she would let traces of her transactions be found."

"But Sherry said the account…"

"Oh! I told Sherry to say that."

Sherry interrupted. "I only agreed because I thought we were on the same side."

Tamara ignored her. "But I had already fired her. You couldn't have known…"

He cut her off. "I knew you would take her back. You give people second chances, and thirds and fourths. You don't give up on people."

Tamara went quiet for a long while, everything was sinking in. The room went dead silent, until the tension in the room made the room too small for all of them.

"The guy who held me hostage—was that you, too? Did you send him after me?"

"I did not. That was Lisa. And that was why I told you to stop looking into this case."

"But… but… how did you know what I was going to do? How…"

"You're a very smart woman, Mara, but before you think, I already thought."

Tamara's shoulder sank. "You could have told me everything. You could have…"

"I couldn't, because I know you wouldn't work with my plan. You would have gone after Lisa. And you would have gotten yourself killed."

Tamara glanced at him and, once again, he seemed like a stranger. She didn't know this man at all. Tears were rolling down her cheeks, her heart breaking into pieces a thousand times over. "You lied to me…"

"That's only because…"

She cut him off. "You used me."

He moved to hold her by the shoulder, but Tamara moved away before he could. "Don't touch me," she said bitterly.

Raymond was quiet, all the anger suddenly disappearing.

"Say something, you idiot!" Tamara yelled, tears in her voice.

He scowled. "What do you want me to say?"

"I don't know," she said and lifted both her arms in a shrug. "That you came back for me just because of your plans. That you used me!"

"If that's the way you want to see this, then, yes, I used you!"

For one stunned moment, Tamara thought she hadn't heard right. She prayed she'd misunderstood; wished that she'd misheard. And then she felt hurt. Her heart ached, broken into a million pieces. Her throat closed up, her body went numb and cold— as cold as stone.

She swallowed and tried to speak past the lumps in her throat. "Screw you," she said coldly, and then turned around and headed for the door.

Raymond followed and softened his voice as he said, "Mara, I'm sorry. Let's not do this."

She turned around and looked him dead in the eyes. "Don't let me ever see you again!"

Opening the front door, she ran out of the room. Raymond's words kept repeating themselves in her mind.

If that's the way you want to see this, then, yes, I used you!

The thought made her heart want to explode, first from the realization that Raymond had lied to her and used her. And second, from the fear of what Lisa could be planning.

Opening the door to her car, Tamara eased herself into the driver's seat. All she wanted right now was to be alone. In a quiet place. Perhaps her house. She just wanted to be alone. She wouldn't cry. She just wanted to clear her head. She wouldn't cry. Raymond wasn't worth her tears anymore.

She cranked the key in the ignition, but before the car could move, she heard a slight knock on her window. She looked to check who it was.

Lisa!

Sighting her, her heart felt as if it would come up to her throat.

And then she leaned on the window and said, "Listen to me, Raymond's dog."

Tamara summoned the strength she didn't know she still had. "Do not call me a dog."

"Oh, but that's what you are," she replied, her voice quiet, almost friendly. "You go around running errands for him, getting things done for him in the hopes that you will one day become Mrs. Connor. Let me advise you like I would if you were my daughter. To Raymond, you're nothing but a cheap, obsessive, lowlife slut, but a smart one. And he's only using you. After all, Raymond is a Connor. We use people to our advantage and dispose of them. That's the Connor way."

Tears filled Tamara's eyes, but she refused to shed it, knowing that nothing would please this monster more than to see her face awash in tears of frustration.

"I guess you must have heard about Dahlia by now. I didn't do that to her, but I promise that I can if I have to. So take my advice, walk away or else I'll rip off your legs and shove them up your ass." She continued to speak quietly. "So let me make myself clear—if you come after my son again, I'm declaring war on you. I'm going to kill you. Horribly. And your mother will wish that you had died at birth."

****

All Tamara wanted to do when she stepped into her house was crawl into bed. But she didn't think she had enough strength to get to the bedroom, so she settled for the couch. Her heart ached so much that she thought she might have a heart attack. Everything she had loved—everything she had known—about Raymond turned out to be false. Raymond lied to her. The evidence was so glaring, staring her in the face, and yet she didn't see it. She failed. She failed because she trusted Raymond so much that she ignored all the possibilities and all the evidence that pointed to him.

She closed her eyes to resist shedding tears. One thing she used to tell her clients was to try as much as possible to never cry for a lost cause. It was high time she started taking her own advice.

Relax. Breathe. Don't cry.

Slowly, she got up from the couch and grabbed a bottle of wine and a glass. Pouring herself a full glass, she gulped it down quickly, poured herself another one and then sat back on the couch. Using the TV remote, she switched on the TV.

Taylor Swift's soft, soulful voice whispered through the speakers into her dimly lit living room. A song about a broken relationship, heartbreak, and how she didn't imagine they'd end like they did.

It sounded like her right now.

She switched off the TV and tried to concentrate her mind on other things. Several things came rushing back and crowded her mind.

If that's the way you want to see this, then, yes, I used you!

To Raymond, you're nothing but a cheap, obsessive, lowlife slut, but a smart one. And he's only using you. After all, Raymond is a Connor. We use people to our advantage and dispose of them. That's the Connor way.

She let out a loud cry, then threw and smashed the emptied glass in her hand against the wall. As the glass broke, it was if the bag of tears inside her had broken, too.

Submitting to the itch, she collapsed on the couch and let the tears flow, whimpering like a little child.

She couldn't tell for how long she had been crying when she heard someone trying to open her door. Only two people had her spare keys—Raymond and Drake.

Lifting her head up from the couch, she tried to see who it was.

"You're adorable when you cry, you know that," he said, a sarcastic look plastered on his face.

Wiping tears off her face, she managed a small smile. "Drake."

Walking over to her, he took a seat beside her on the couch. "Look, let me take a picture of you, and I'll show you."

She let out a frustrated sigh and looked away.

"Look at me. You look like this when you cry." He squeezed his face into a silly, ugly ball. Tamara couldn't help but give a small laugh even amidst her tears.

And then he held her by the waist and drew her closer to himself. She let her head rest on his strong chest.

"He was such an asshole back there," he said, his voice low and gentle as he stroked her already tangled hair.

Head still on his chest, she tried to look at him and nodded in agreement.

And then he slowly wiped her tears with his thumb.

For a long time, he said nothing.

He just kept staring at her.

Face to face as though it was the most natural thing in the world, he leaned closer and kissed her forehead so gently at first that she melted. His breath was warm and soothing, the feel of his lips soft and tender on her skin, and his scent, strong and masculine with a soft hint of *trust me, I won't hurt you.*

When he stopped, he looked at her face so their lips lined up, his eyes asking her if she wanted more. She didn't know if she did, but before she could make up her mind, he took her mouth in a deep, passionate kiss.

She responded hungrily, giving up, losing herself. His hands slipped under her top and her nipple hardened in anticipation of his hand over her breast.

This was Drake, her longtime friend. If they did this, there would be no going back.

He tilted his head, leaned closer, intensifying the kiss, and she let her hands glide over his arms and back. His muscles were strong, hardening under the pressure of her hand. He released her mouth shortly, only to place hot, fiery kisses on her cheeks and neck while his hands tugged at her top.

Her blouse was about to be history. And soon she'd feel the touch of his warm hands on her bare skin. Her body shivered in anticipation.

"Wait," she said softly and swallowed.

Slowly he lifted his head, revealing eyes naked with passion. "Wait? Okay?" He relaxed a bit, giving her a look that said wait for what.

She couldn't say a thing. She lacked the words right now and couldn't even manage to look at him.

Without a word, he drew her close and held her tightly in his arms.

"You still love him, don't you?"

She tried not to nod, but he was damn right. Raymond had become a part of her. No matter who he was, what he did and what he said, she'd always love him.

Releasing herself from his hold, she looked at him. "You should go."

He nodded. "I will, but from now on, I doubt I'll ever be able to see you and not have X-rated thoughts about you."

Her lips curved into a gentle smile. "You've always had X-rated thoughts about me."

He smiled back and lifted an arm in a shrug. "Maybe."

The moment passed, and he hugged her again. "Are you going to be alright?"

It took her more than a second to mumble a response. "I don't know."

"You'll be alright," he assured her.

Tamara nodded, and then he stood up. "I should go, before the X-rated thoughts become too explicit."

She stood up, nodded and smiled.

He hugged her again and then was gone.

After he left, Tamara thought of going to bed and peacefully falling asleep. But then she decided against it, because she knew that if she did, she'd crash and might not get out of bed for the next three days. It had become a habit for her. Whenever her heart was broken, she'd stayed in bed till she felt relieved.

But she knew she couldn't afford to crash—not until she found out what Lisa was up to.

She got herself a blanket, made herself comfortable on the couch and tried to force herself to sleep.

****

Raymond cranked the key in the ignition and pulled onto the street. He drove speedily toward Mara's house.

What was I thinking? What the hell did I do that for? Mara has been looking out for me, trying to save me, and the first thing I do is be ungrateful and spite her for it, he thought. It was his fault, after all. If he had told her the whole truth—if he hadn't hidden anything from her— she wouldn't have made the mistake.

All he was trying to do was protect her. If he had told her he knew it was Lisa. Mara would have gone after Lisa, and Lisa would have killed her, the same way she killed James Connor's lawyer and Dahlia.

All he wanted to do was use Joe to bring Lisa to the table, so he could try to make peace with her and cut a deal. He believed that when the devil was after your meal, you don't fight her—you just prepare her a meal, too.

He parked his car in front of Tamara's house and got in. He noticed another car parked there, but he didn't pay attention. He was preoccupied with

Mara—getting to her, apologizing, telling her that he didn't mean what he said.

He walked toward the front door and his eyes reflexively darted through the window. What he saw almost took his breath away. Mara! In Drake's arms. Kissing him with a kind of passion that he recognized; a passion that should only be for him.

How long have they been doing this behind my back? How long have they made a fool out of me? Such a fool I've been.

Anger built up within him, rising to his throat as if it would choke him to death. His breath became so shallow that he was afraid he'd suffocate if he didn't relax. He quickly unclenched his fist before he rushed into the house and beat the man to a stupor.

When the sight was too much to behold, he ran back to his car and sped home. As he drove, several thoughts rushed through his mind that only made him assume the worst.

When he got into his house, he poured himself a drink and sank into his couch. The more he thought of it, the more his anger grew.

Did she choose Drake over him? He wouldn't blame her if she did. Drake was capable of making her happy, giving her a life without drama, a life where she didn't have to look over her shoulder in fear of someone trying to kill her. No messy marriage, no baby drama. He was perfect for her.

He tried so hard not to think about it, to shut his heart to Mara, to forget Mara, never to remember her again.

Trying to put his mind on other things, he noticed the house was quiet. Dahlia was gone, and

Lisa had taken Richard from him since she found out that Richard was her grandson. The house was quiet, and he could feel the crushing loneliness the house held.

In a way, he missed Richard, even though he had always known the baby wasn't his. He loved him. And he missed Dahlia, too, the woman he had once despised. Dahlia might be greedy and let herself be used by Lisa, but in her own way, she must have loved him. He just had to believe that. He was trying to think good of the dead no matter how hard it seemed.

EIGHTEEN

The conference room was dead silent as Tamara walked in. After Raymond publicly confirmed their affair at the party, she wasn't expecting clients to flood in like they used to, but that was okay.

Raymond had used her, so it wasn't a bad idea if she used him, too. She was going to accept the million dollar office building he bought her. She would continue her life, her career. Not that the building was enough for all the love she gave him. In fact, some women would have considered it an honorable thing if she rejected it and let him know she couldn't be bought off after being used. But that would have been foolish on her part, and it was time to stop being foolish.

"After what happened yesterday, you must all think that we failed," she began as she eased herself into the chair and rested her elbows on the table. "Well, let me tell you that we didn't fail, and the battle has only just begun." Her eyes darted sharply to Sherry. "And Sherry, I haven't forgotten that you helped Raymond throw away this investigation..."

"I swear, I only agreed to help because I thought we were on the same side," she replied, her voice truly remorseful.

"Next time, if anybody wants you to do something, and I don't know about it, then the person is definitely not on my side."

She nodded. "Okay. Does it mean you're not going to fire me?"

"I don't know," she replied, and then took her concentration back to everyone, raising her voice as she said boldly, "We're going after Lisa Connor!"

Pausing, she glanced at their faces. Sherry had fear plastered on her face, Megan had doubt and confusion, and Drake's face was blank, totally expressionless.

"She's dangerous," Megan said.

"Not too dangerous," Drake countered.

"She killed Dahlia just to clean up a mess."

"I'm going to kill you. Horribly. And your mother will wish that you had died at birth," Tamara said. And her words threw them into a dark hole of confusion. "That was Lisa threatening me outside the hospital yesterday. So I agree with you, she is dangerous. And that's why I wouldn't hold anything against anyone who doesn't want to be a part of this."

Silence covered the room.

She glanced at Drake. "Drake?"

"You know I'll gladly jump in front of a moving train for you. All you have to do is ask."

Her gaze went to Sherry. "Sherry?"

She nodded. "I'm in."

"Me, too," Megan said before Tamara could ask her.

"Good," Tamara replied. "Megan and Sherry, I want you to go over all the files we have on the

Connor case. See if we missed anything." She looked at Drake. "Drake, come with me. We've got work to do."

He stood from his chair. "You do know that we don't stand a chance against Lisa, right?"

Tamara stood up and started to walk toward the door. "Yes. And that's why we are going to ask for somebody's help. Someone who knew her longer than most."

"Who is this person? Where are we going?"

"Wolvestream Correctional Facility."

****

"Rachel Brock,"

Tamara called as she walked into the small room. Rachel Brock sat in front of a small desk, surprise and confusion clearly written on her face. She sat up tall, so Tamara knew she wasn't a short woman. She was slim and dark-skinned; her face daring and strong and her scanty hair held up in ponytail. She looked much younger than Tamara had imagined. From her profile, she was supposed to be in her late fifties, but she sure as hell looked ten years younger. Despite having been in jail the last twenty years, she did age well. Seeing her, Tamara could tell where Raymond got his strong, charming eyes.

"My name is Tamara Price, and this is Drake Johnson," she said, pointing to Drake standing next to her. "Mr. Johnson is going to be representing you in court because, in light of new evidence, we will be resurrecting your case."

Her big brown eyes went wide. "What evidence?"

Tamara took a seat opposite her and Drake sat in the chair next to Tamara.

Drake slightly leaned on the table, staring hard into her eyes. "I'm aware that you confessed to the crime, but we have reasons to believe that you didn't do it. That you didn't try to poison James Connor. So, we're going to appeal your case on the basis that your confession was made under duress. Someone threatened you. You were afraid for your life and the life of your family, and you made the confession that took twenty years out of your life." He paused to make sure she understood him, searching her eyes. "It might not look like enough to build your hopes around it, but I'm telling you that it's enough because I'm good at what I do. I've represented criminals that were caught in the act, and they've walked. Not that that was a good thing, I'm just telling you how well I do my job."

Rachel heaved a deep sigh. "Why?" she asked. Her voice was soft, so tender that Tamara kind of felt the confirmation that this woman was incapable of hurting a fly. "Not that I don't appreciate you trying to help, but why? Did Raymond put you up to this? Did my son hire you to help me?"

"No," Tamara replied.

She watched Rachel shift uneasily in her chair and swallow hard. "Then why?"

Tamara placed her hand on the table and leaned closer, her voice gentle and trustworthy. "Because I need your help."

"What can I do for you?"

"Lisa Connor. You know her, right?"

She nodded.

"Well, Lisa is about to destroy everything, including your son. She tried to poison him, but thank goodness I knew about it soon. And now he's taking treatment. But his wife, Dahlia and wasn't that lucky. Lisa killed her and now she has threatened to come after me and Raymond. Rachel, you've known Lisa longer than most. You must know something about her that will help me get to her. Maybe a weakness or someone you know is capable of making Lisa see reason."

Rachel heaved another sigh, shifted in her seat and rested her hands on the table. She didn't give a response.

"Rachel, are you going to help me?" Tamara asked.

Rachel nodded. "On one condition."

"Name it. Anything."

Rachel looked her straight in the eye. "I want to see my son."

Tamara betrayed no emotion, but continued to hold her gaze. "That's not possible. I don't have that kind of access to your son."

"Of course, you do. I know you, Tamara Price. I know what relationship you have with my son."

She pulled her brows together. "How?"

"He announced it loud and clear at the anniversary party." She glanced at Tamara. "Do you think I have no idea of what goes on in the world because I'm locked up?"

"Still… Raymond made it clear that he didn't want to see you. It's going to take more time to convince him to come here."

Her voice hardened. "I don't care. Bring my son to me or else I won't help you."

****

Raymond eased his black Ferrari into his garage and stepped out. He wasn't exactly sure, but he thought he saw someone that looked like Mara. Maybe his mind was playing games with him. She tried to come into his office today, and he had told security men not to let her in. He had given the same order to the men who guarded his home. Mara was not to be allowed within 10 feet of him or his property.

"RAYMOND!" Anger flared in her voice as she walked over.

But whatever she was angry at, it could in no way compare to what he was feeling right now. "What do you want?"

"I called you like a thousand times, but you didn't pick my call. I tried to come see you at the office, but you told security not to let me in." She stopped a few strides away from him, probably to prevent things from getting personal.

"Oh, I gave the same orders to the men at my house. I wonder why they're not doing their jobs. Let me guess—did you seduce them into…"

She scowled and cut him off. "What is your problem?"

"What's my problem?"

She glared at him, her chest heaving. "Yes. What is your problem? I'm the one that should be angry right now. You're the one who lied to me. You're the one who got me confused. I don't even know who you are anymore. You knew Anita betrayed you, yet you kept working with her, laughing with her as if nothing was wrong. That is a dangerous attribute for anyone to have. And you knew about Dahlia and Dr. Morgan, but you influenced me so you could pin it all on Joe just so you could draw his mother out and reason with her? It sounds to me like you pinned everything on Joe just so you could send him away and have all the Connor wealth to yourself."

"I don't care what you think. Get out of my house."

She felt like a bucket of cold water had been dumped on her.

"What?"

"You heard me. Get out of my house."

"Ray?"

"I said get out of my house!" he growled, pointing back to the gate.

The anger in his eyes scared her, and she shuddered. She walked closer; gazing into his deep brown eyes, she saw that he had closed his heart to her. She got a grip on her own anger and regrouped. She wasn't going to leave without getting what she came for. "Lisa threatened me."

"Lisa is no longer a threat. The police have discovered that the evidence against Joe was false, so I got him released. I've made a deal with Lisa. She wants Joe to be part of the board of directors and for me to help bring Josh back home from Europe. If I do all that, Lisa won't be a problem anymore."

"You don't actually believe her, do you? Lisa is always going to want more. She is..." Pausing, she decided against speaking further and cut to the chase. "Your mother wants to see you."

"What? You went to see my mom?"

"Yes, and she's agreed to help me fight Lisa, but she has to see you before she will give me any info."

"I made it clear—I don't want anything to do with that woman!"

"I think she didn't do it. Drake thinks he can appeal her case on the basis that her confession was under duress."

"So it's you and Drake again. You two still screwing, huh?"

She stood frozen. The innocent, confused look on her face made his heart want to explode with anger. That was it. In a blink, he was a few strides closer to her, staring at her, glaring down at her.

"Don't give me that innocent look!" he yelled. "I saw you. I came to your place, worried about you, to apologize, and I saw you. You and him." He paused for a brief second, and his glare deepened. "How long have you two been screwing? How long?" he barked.

By her expression, the memory obviously pained her as it did him. In a split second, tears gathered in her eyes. Something struck at his heart. How he hated to see her cry. He wanted to curse himself for being the reason behind her tears.

Opening her mouth, she tried to speak, to say something, but nothing came out. She shut her mouth and glanced away. When she glanced back at him, she sniffled back her tears and tried to say something. "V..." she stammered amidst sobs that she was trying so hard to suppress. "Vegas... Palms Place Hotel," was all she managed to say.

He flipped through his mental files. He sure as hell couldn't forget Palms Place Hotel in Las Vegas. The trip to Vegas was their very first trip together, and they stayed at the Palms Place Hotel. It was in Vegas that he brought himself to admit that he was in love with Mara. He had known quite a lot of women before Tamara. Women passed through his life in large numbers, and he'd bedded more than his fair share. He never took the same woman to bed twice. Only once, and he was done. But Mara, she affected him. Made him feel different, and he never stopped wanting her. More and more, until it almost drove him to insanity. He thought it weird, but Mara was his first love and definitely his last.

He not only admitted it to himself, but to Mara. After Mara, there could be no one else. He could still remember telling her, *the love I have for you taught me how to be content with only one woman.* Those were his exact words. If Mara was reminding him of that, she was saying...

Dammit! He wanted to beat himself up right there.

He looked at her, silent tears streaming down her eyes, the hurt in her alluring, brown eyes filling him with anger and resentment at himself.

"I tried..." she said, sniffing back her tears. "But I couldn't. After you, I can't just be with anyone else. I can't... I can't." Her voice faded away and she glanced at the ground.

He clenched and unclenched his fist as he watched her shoulders shaking as she wept.

"It was only a kiss, and it meant nothing," she said softly. And then she glanced back at him. "I forgive everything you ever did. Can't you forgive me this one time? This one time, can't you…"

He cut her off with a kiss on her lips. It took her by surprise, but she didn't stop him. Holding her face with both hands, he deepened the kiss. It soothed her, as if that was all she needed. She pressed close against him, curling her arms around his neck and tumbling into pure sensation.

He felt himself stirred into hardness. When he broke the kiss, he held her gaze, the awareness and the fire in her eyes matching his own. And he knew that she was definitely as aroused as he was.

Ever so gently, he carried her in his arms like a baby into his house and into his bedroom.

They had never made love in his house, in his room, on his bed. They stood next to the bed as his hand reached behind her head to undo the knot of her hair, letting it spill over her shoulder. Never taking his eyes away from her, he helped her lift her dress over her head while she undressed him until he stood naked before her as she stood before him.

When they lay down on his bed, he moved with her so slowly that time seemed to have stopped.

She had never felt better than she did that day as Raymond slowly made love to her, his hands adoring her, his eyes telling her louder than words that he loved her. He told her that everything was perfect only when she was there, and his kiss on her

trembling skin told her of something more than sex.
As she fell asleep, he held her in his arms.

NINETEEN

"I'm doing this because of you," Raymond said as they walked past the last security checkpoint.

"And I'm grateful," she replied. "But one day, you will have to forgive her because I think she didn't do it."

"I appreciate that you're trying to see the good in her, but I'm absolutely certain she did do it."

"Even if she did, she's been jailed for twenty years. I think she has suffered enough for it."

The door opened and Raymond saw his mother sitting right in front of a small desk waiting for him. Twenty years. It had been twenty years since he last saw this woman. How old was he then? Thirteen or fourteen? He had grown into manhood alone, without the love and care of his parents, without their guidance.

And seeing his mother right now, he thought he should feel anger toward her for everything she did. But he felt... he felt nothing. He wasn't angry and he wasn't too happy.

"Raymond," her monotone voice broke through his reverie.

And then he allowed himself to actually look at her. She looked older than the last time he saw her.

Her once bright eyes were dull, as if she had seen too much suffering. A part of him felt sympathy for her and another part of him thought she got what she deserved. Still. no matter how bad she was, no matter what crime she might have committed, she was his mother.

"Mom." He managed to get the words out.

Slowly, he took a seat opposite her and right next to Mara.

"You've grown into such a fine man," she said softly, her eyes roaming over him, truly admiring the man he had grown into.

Raymond didn't reply. His only response was a smile and a small nod.

"I heard what happened to Dahlia, your wife. I'm so sorry."

He shook his head slowly. "Don't be sorry. It's not your fault."

Leaning forward, she placed her hands over Ray's, looking intently into his eyes. "You don't understand, child, there's so many things I should apologize for. I'm sorry for taking the law into my hands, I'm sorry for trying to kill your father. You hated me so much for it. And most of all, I'm sorry that I wasn't there for you, that I wasn't there to see you grow up, that I wasn't there to make you nice meals, to bake you cakes and cookies, to mend your torn clothes. I'm sorry for all the birthdays that I missed. I'm sorry I wasn't at your graduation..." Tears filled her eyes and she held his hand tighter. "I'm sorry I wasn't..."

"Mom!" he said, trying to stop her.

"You don't understand. I'm sorry for..."

His heart went out to her. He couldn't bear to see her cry. She was sorry, that was enough. All the anger he had kept toward her suddenly melted away. "Mom, it's okay."

She held his hands to her mouth and kissed it. "I really am sorry."

"I'm sorry, too," he said, struggling to get the words out. "I shouldn't have abandoned you here. I should have tried..."

"Don't blame yourself, Raymond. You did the right thing. I deserve what I got."

He held back his tears like a real man and held her hand firmly. "We could get another chance. Mara thinks she can get you out of here. She's good at what she does. I'm going to support her, do everything in my power, give it everything I have. I will get you out of here and maybe we can give it another try, you know, this mother-and-son thing."

She smiled, but she shook her head gently. "No, Raymond. I've chosen my own path; forged a new path for myself. I deserve what I got. I belong here."

"Mom! The sentence you got wasn't fair. You only tried to kill him, but you didn't. Twenty years is more than enough to serve as penance for that, don't you think?"

"No, son. At least not in the eyes of the law."

He lowered his head in frustration.

"You're a good son, Raymond, and it's enough for me that I get to see you again."

Tamara cleared her throat to get their attention. "I hate to cut short the reunion, but we don't have much time. Rachel, please, if there's anything you know that can help me fight Lisa, now is the time."

Rachel slowly let go of Raymond's hand, and then wiped a tear from her eyes. "When I was working for Lisa, there was this guy that always came looking for her. I think he does her dirty jobs. If you can find this guy, I'm sure he will have more info about all the dirty jobs he did for Lisa. And if she tried to feed Raymond some arsenic, I'm sure this guy is her source. He almost certainly got it for her."

"Good. Do you have a name?"

"Yes. His name is Kyle Chapelle, but I don't have an address for him." She dropped her face in disappointment.

"You were helpful enough. I can get an address for him."

"Glad to help. Get Kyle, and you get Lisa."

****

When they got back to the parking lot, Tamara reached for her purse and grabbed her cellphone. She made a quick call to Drake.

"Hey, Drake, still friends with your guys in the Feds?"

"Hell, yeah," Drake replied.

"Good, because Rachel Brock just gave a name, and we need an address for him."

"What's the name?"

"Kyle Chapelle."

"Okay, I'll get back to you asap."

She hung up and then glanced at Raymond, her brow wrinkled together in confusion. "You know, I'm worried about something."

"What?" Ray asked.

"The first time I talked to your mother, I mentioned that Lisa was trying to kill you, but I never mentioned that she was trying to do it with arsenic. Back in there, she mentioned something about it. I wonder how she knew."

Raymond raised an eyebrow. "What do you think? You think…"

Tamara cut him off and quickly dismissed the idea. "No, it might be nothing."

He stopped walking and looked at Mara, staring intently into her eyes. "Still, your first intuition is almost always right. What do you think?"

"I think I'm being paranoid. When you collapsed at the anniversary party, the media made a big deal out of it. They talked about the possibility that you were poisoned. Your mother must have picked it up from the news."

Raymond shrugged and resumed walking.

By the time they walked to the car, her phone signaled that she had a text. She read through it very quickly and then glanced at Raymond. "Looks like I have a long trip ahead of me. Kyle Chapelle recently moved to Chicago."

"We have a long trip ahead of us," he corrected.

She gave him a questioning look. "We?"

He nodded. "Yes, we. I'm not going to let you do this alone anymore." He didn't wait for her response. Grabbing his phone, he made a quick call to Tamara didn't know who. "Hey, prepare Lily for travel, please. I've got urgent business in Chicago."

Of course, Lily was the Connor's private jet, the one she had been dreaming of flying in for a long time now.

Her eyes went wide. "Really? We can fly Lily to Chicago?"

He nodded, smiling. "I wanted the first time to be to our honeymoon, but seeing that we have need of it..." He shrugged.

She rolled her eyes at him. "Planning our honeymoon, and you haven't even popped the question yet."

His eyes went wide. "Planning my future with you, and you still don't know that I'm asking you to marry me."

"There's just something about a man getting on his knees and popping the question that makes me... you know."

He smiled and shook his head. "See what happens when women watch too many romance movies."

****

Two hours later, they were in Chicago.

Everything was still around Kyle's little apartment. They saw no sign that Kyle was home. No car parked in front of the house. No lights on.

Tamara knocked on the door, gently at first, then harder and louder later on.

"He's not here," Raymond said.

Still, Tamara kept knocking. When she heard no response, something prompted her to open the door. Slowly, she placed her hand on the knob and realized the door wasn't locked. Applying a little force, she pushed open the door.

The sight she beheld almost took her breath away.

Kyle's body lay lifelessly on the floor. Was he really dead? He couldn't be. He had to be alive. How could he possibly die? But the blood... There was blood all around, streaming from his wrist. His wrist had been cut, but by whom?

Cold bumps ran up her arms. Putting her hand over her mouth, she tried to stifle a scream.

By now, Raymond was already kneeling next to Kyle, his hand on his neck checking to see if he had a pulse.

He glanced back at Tamara. "Call 911!"

His tense voice brought her out of shock. Very quickly, she grabbed her phone from inside her purse and made the call.

In the absence of gauze, Raymond grabbed a shirt that was on the couch and wrapped it around Kyle's wrist, pressing it down, applying pressure as he tried to control the bleeding.

While they waited for the ambulance, Tamara's eye caught a small note lying beside Kyle's body. She squatted, picked up the note and read through it very quickly.

"Suicide note," she said as she lifted her face and looked at Raymond.

"He tried to kill himself?"

She shook her head. "Someone tried to kill him and made it look like suicide."

"But..." he stuttered. "How could you possibly know that?"

"I just know," she replied, her eyes scanning the room again. Something had to be here. Something that could help her find the person who did this. Her heart was racing fast. The ambulance. The cops would be here any second and once they arrived, she'd no longer have access to the scene.

Focus!

She chided herself and tried to pay full attention to the scene. His cellphone!

Her eyes caught his cellphone lying on the floor close to the body. Quickly, she opened her purse, grabbed a handkerchief and picked up his cell. She looked through it, but all she saw were some dialed numbers. She felt prompted to call back the last number that he dialed. She typed the number into her phone and dialed.

You've reached Ben Murray. Leave me a detailed message, and I'll get back to you.

Her head spun around.

Before her mind could respond to what she had just heard, the ambulance siren blasted out at full volume, followed by flashes of blue and red. Tamara quickly dropped the phone.

In a split second, Kyle was stretched into the ambulance while tons of police officers covered the crime scene.

Tamara and Raymond were interrogated for a firsthand account of what happened at the scene.

And when the police finally let them go, she grabbed her phone to make a quick call.

"Who are you calling?" Raymond asked.

"When I approached Dr. Morgan about the money in his account, he told me that a man paid him the money and asked him not to diagnose you correctly. At the time, my thought was that the man was Joe. Maybe…"

Dr. Morgan's voice came through the phone. "Tamara?"

"Yes, Dr. Morgan. When I approached you about Dahlia sending money to your account, you said it wasn't Dahlia. You said it was a man."

"And I told you that I never met him."

"But you spoke to him on the phone, correct?"

"Yes."

"Would you recognize his voice if you heard it again?"

"Yes, of course."

"I'll text you a number right now. Call this number and let me know if that's the voice of the man who called you."

She hung up and quickly sent the phone number to him in a text. They got into their rented car and drove to the airport where they had parked Lily.

A few minutes later, Dr. Morgan called back.

"It's him?" Tamara asked.

"Yes, it's him."

"Are you sure?"

"Absolutely. I couldn't forget his baritone voice."

"Well, thanks for your help."

She hung up and glanced at Raymond. "It's him."

Raymond hit the steering wheel with his fist, murmuring a curse under his breath.

"All this while, I thought it was Lisa."

"I still think it is Lisa," Tamara replied. "But Ben might be working with her."

With a moan of frustration, Raymond sagged his back on the seat, trying to focus on the road. Everyone around him, everyone close to him, had betrayed him. Dahlia, Anita, Dr. Morgan and Ben. He was angry, confused and frustrated. He wanted so much for this nightmare to be over.

His phone vibrated inside his suit jacket, bringing him out of his thoughts. Reaching inside his suit jacket, he grabbed his phone and tried to see who it was. And then his gaze slowly went to Mara.

"Who's calling?" Tamara asked.

"Ben. A video call through Skype."

Raymond considered for a while, and then accepted the call, putting on his friendly but commanding tone, one he usually reserved for clients. "Ben, I'm out of town right now. You can handle any business till I get back."

"This isn't business, Raymond. It's something else."

"Well, Ben, I know it's late. So why don't you go home for now? We'll discuss everything that is not business when I get back from this trip," he replied, glancing at his phone once in a while and quickly taking his gaze back to the road.

Ben gave a low laugh. "I've got someone that you will very well like to meet."

Raymond watched as the camera shifted. When the camera landed on the person he wanted him to see, something went through Raymond like a bolt of lightning. Rage and belated fear surged through Raymond all at once. Anger flashed in his eyes.

"What is it?" Tamara asked, and then leaned in to take a peep at the phone. "Momma!" she yelled. "Let her go, you son of a bitch!"

He didn't respond and Tamara kept looking at the video. Her mother was tied to a chair, looking rough and tattered, her hands bound and mouth taped to prevent her from crying for help.

Her mother was in going through hell because of her, because she got involved with the sharks. Hot tears gathered in her eyes and she tried to swallow back the tears, running her hands through her hair in frustration.

Ben took the camera back to himself, retaining the smirk on his face. "Still think we will discuss this when you get back?"

"Alright, Ben," he replied, trying to even his voice. "You got me. You got my attention. Let her go, and I'll pretend this never happened."

"You don't call the shots any more, Raymond. I do."

"Okay. What do you want?" he asked, trying as much as possible to hide his fear and anger.

"You love Tamara very much, right? I don't think she will feel the same way about you if you let her mother die."

"What do you want?"

"You. If you want her back, I want you. I give you two hours to get back from your trip and bring yourself to me. Alert the cops, and she's dead."

He hung up.

Raymond threw his phone on the center console of the car and hit the steering wheel again.

Tamara, on the other hand, was quiet, almost calm. She was devastated. And even though she was doing a very good job of not showing her worries and fears, she was barely keeping a lid on it on the inside.

Grabbing her cell, she made another call to Drake.

"Hey, Tamara..."

She cut off his pleasantries and got to the point. "It's Ben..." Her voice broke off, but she tried to keep it steady.

"What?"

"Yes, it's been Ben all the while. I'm not sure if he's working for Lisa, but the son of a bitch's got my momma!"

"Oh, no!"

"I need you to get me every bit of info on Ben. Anything you can get your hands on. I need them ASAP."

"Okay. How soon?"

"Like yesterday."

"Tamara, I can't get it that fast. It will take me at least 24 hours to make all the calls."

She stopped talking and glanced at Raymond. "Ray, you have to help. You must know people that can help..."

He cut her off. "I'll make a few calls."

She nodded, and took her attention back to Drake. "Drake, you there?"

"Yes."

"Tell Megan to help you with anything you need, and tell Sherry to alert the police."

"You really want to get the cops involved?"

She ignored his question. "Tell her to show them all the evidence we have."

"What do you want her to tell the police?"

She went quiet for a while, considering if she really wanted to do this. And then she swallowed hard and said, "The truth. Let her tell the whole truth from the beginning."

"Okay."

She hung up.

For one very long second, there was a dead silent in the car. Tamara's face was calm, her eyes glued to the road ahead of them.

But Raymond had known her long enough to know that her face might be calm, but there was trouble, pain and hurt brewing inside her.

"Mara..."

She cut him off, but didn't look at him. "I'm okay, if that's what you want to ask. I'm holding up okay. Ben won't kill my mother. He wants you. He wants you, and my mother is his leverage. He won't kill her, or else he has nothing on you. He will keep her alive. The question is, for how long?"

Raymond let out a deep breath. "I was going to ask you why you reached out to the police."

This time, she took her eyes off the road and looked at him. "Someone very dear to me once told me not to be ashamed to ask for help when I'm helpless."

Raymond nodded slowly and swallowed hard. Never before had he heard Mara admit to being helpless. She always found a way out of trouble. Seeing her admit to being helpless made his heart ache, all the more so because it was his fault.

Briefly taking his eyes off the road, he looked at her and held her hand. "I won't let anything happen to your mother. I'll give it my last breath if I have to."

She looked at him and nodded slowly.

TWENTY

One hour thirty minutes later, they were back in Baltimore. The flight should be exactly one hour thirty minutes, but the pilot was able to push it to one hour twenty minutes. And it took ten minutes to drive from the airport back to Connor Corp.

When Raymond parked his car in the executive parking area, they were welcomed by Drake, Megan and Sherry.

"Tamara, are you okay?" Megan asked with a concerned voice.

"I'm okay," she replied and glanced at Drake. "You got anything for me?"

"Sure," he replied and handed her a folder. "Contains every bit of info I could gather in the last hour. Phone records, emails…"

Tamara took her attention to Raymond. "I need access to Ben's office, his computer and everything he owns."

"No problem," Raymond said, He led them to the elevator and pressed the button for the 8th floor. Still in the elevator, Tamara opened the folder and tried to read through it quickly. Her heart was racing. She didn't know exactly what she was looking for. Anything. Just anything that could give her a hint of what Ben was going to do to her momma. If she died this way, she wouldn't forgive herself. It was her fault. If she had stayed away from Raymond—if she didn't start the affair with Ray after he married Dahlia—her mother would be safe right now.

The elevator stopped on the 8th floor, and they all stepped out, Tamara still not taking her eyes away from the opened folder in her hands.

Before Raymond could open the door to Ben's office, Tamara's head snapped up and glanced at Drake, raising a brow. "Talktech is an inmate phone service provider, correct?" she asked, holding her breath, trying to pray that she was wrong.

"Yes. Talktech has been around for a long time now."

A deep sigh escaped from in between her lips. "Oh, no!"

"What?" they chorused.

"Ben..." she began. "He's been using Talktech a lot in the last few months. It makes sense." She could barely look at Raymond. "She's the only one in prison that..."

Tamara's words felt like a punch to Raymond, and he staggered a bit, resting on Ben's office door for support.

Rachel.

Ben was working with Rachel.

It had been Rachel all the while. Rachel was the one who placed Dahlia into his life. Rachel was the one who turned everybody, including Anita, against him. His mother was the one who ordered that he be poisoned. Rachel was the one who called the shots over Dahlia's death just to keep her from talking. And she was certainly the one who gave the order to kidnap Mara's mother just to get to him. His insides turned to ice.

Raymond could manage only a whisper. "My mother..."

"It doesn't make any sense," Tamara said, her voice tense. "Why would your mother want you dead?"

"You remember when I told you that I'm more than certain that my mother did try to kill James Connor?"

She nodded.

"Well, this is how I knew." He swallowed hard. "I saw her. I was fourteen or fifteen at the time. I got back from school and went to the Connor's mansion to stay with my mom. I always did that after school. And that day, I saw her pouring this substance into the tea that had been prepared for James. It wasn't only her confession that sent her to jail. I stood as a witness against her."

He glanced around and could see the surprise on their faces. He felt the need to finish his story. "After she went to jail, I had no one. James rejected me, and I went from one foster home to the other."

Raymond suppressed his emotions and made a quick assessment of the situation. The only thing that mattered now was getting Mara's mother back. If he lost himself now, she would be the one to suffer; she would be the one at Rachel's mercy.

Raymond pulled his key card out of his pocket and opened the door. When he walked into the office, he glanced around. Everything looked normal. And then he slowly walked to the table and to his computer, trying to override his password.

Everybody else started looking around, opening drawers, for any hints of Ben's plan. After a few moment of searching, Drake's voice boomed through the room. "Tamara, you have to see this."

Tamara walked over to him, took the paper from him and began to unfold it. When she was done, she had to place the paper on the table, looking intently at the drawings on it. After a short moment, she sighed and slowly sank to the chair.

"What is this?" Sherry asked, looking as confused as everyone else.

Tamara slowly replied; "The schematics of Wolvestream Correctional Facility."

Drake glanced around. "There could be only one explanation. He's going to break Rachel Brock out of jail."

Tamara suppressed her emotions, cleared her head and rose to her feet. "Drake, please, contact the Wolvestream…"

She stopped talking when she heard the door open. Glancing at the door, she checked to see who it was. She was surprise when he saw Joe Connor walk into the office. Not that she was surprised to see him, but she wasn't prepared to see him just yet. Not after she handed him over to the police by mistake.

"You have to see this," he said, walking over to the TV. He switched it on and increased the volume.

BREAKING NEWS: Two Wolvestream inmates broke out of jail….

****

The moment passed and Tamara glanced around, suddenly noticing that Raymond was gone.

"Where's Raymond?"

"He was just here," Sherry said. "His phone rang and…"

"Dammit!" Tamara yelled, reaching for her cell and making a quick call to Raymond. As soon as she heard a click, she said, "Ray, where are you?"

There was a long moment of silence, and then he said, "Ben called. Gave me an address. I'm going to give myself to him in exchange for your mother."

"Ray, you're not thinking right. How are you sure they're going to let you and my momma go?"

"This is the only way to get your mother back alive. There is no other way."

"There is always another way," she replied with a sense of urgency. "Drake's talking to the police. He said they have strong intel on Rachel's location. They will find Rachel and get my mother back, I know!"

"Since when did you trust the police?"

It was her turn to be quiet. When she finally found her voice, she struggled to get the words out. "Ever since I realized that I can't do it all myself. I can't do it all alone." She never had to admit it before, but this series of event had taught her that.

"This whole mess started because of me, Mara. I have to put an end to it."

"What do you think you're doing?" Her voice was loud and harsh, but she didn't care. She was getting angry now. "Rachel and Ben have tried to kill you how many times now? You actually think they're going to let you go and release my mother just like that?"

"Mara, I have to…"

She cut him off. "You don't have to do anything," she yelled, shaking with impotent anger. "You have nothing to prove by doing this, Ray. She's your mother, but she will kill you. She will kill you," she repeated again, as if the realization of the imminent of death would make him change his mind.

"Mara…" was all the response he could give.

She knew he wouldn't change his mind. Raymond could be very determined. She lacked the words to convince him and tears gathered in her eyes. "Ray," she said, her voice shaky. "You know when you said I never used to say I love you as much as you expected." He didn't respond, but she continued, strongly believing he was listening. "The reason I don't say it too often is because I thought I would be letting my guard down if I say I love you to a man who is married to another woman. But the truth is, I love you, Ray." She paused and swallowed. "I love you too too much, more than anything. I'm nothing without you, Ray. If you die, you end me."

He didn't respond. Silence roared in her ears. A few seconds later, she heard him sniffing back tears. "Mara," his voice was low, and Tamara had to concentrate to hear him. "I love you from my soul. I love you more than life itself."

He loved her more than life itself.

She knew what that meant.

She shut her eyes and grimaced like she was in pain. "Ray, please don't do this," she pleaded, tears in her voice.

He was quiet for a long time, and then he hung up.

Immediately after Raymond hung up, Tamara felt as if she had just been hit by a moving train. All she could think about was how to help rescue Raymond and her mother.

Hands on her waist, she paced back and forth, her heart heaving in her chest. After some seconds, she glanced around, her eyes scanning all of their faces. "When Ben video-called Raymond, I saw a CC logo CC on the walls of the house where my mother was held."

"So we know that Ben is holding your mother hostage at a Connor Corp facility," Drake said.

Tamara nodded and then glanced at Joe. "Joe, can I have a list of all properties owned by Connor Corp in the Baltimore area?"

"Sure," he replied and walked over to sit in front of the computer. After some seconds, he turned the monitor to Tamara.

Before Tamara could respond, Drake interrupted. "Nah! She doesn't do computers. Has to be in papers."

"Really?"

Tamara nodded.

"Wow! That means we've got plenty work to do," he said, trying to print the screen. The printer didn't work so he walked out of the office. After a few minutes, he returned with a box full of documents. "So what are we looking for?" he asked as he dropped the box on the floor.

"I don't know," Tamara replied. "Anything unusual."

Taking off her heels, she sat on the floor and began reading through all the documents. Megan, Drake and Sherry joined her.

After about five minutes of frustrated reading, Sherry angrily dropped the last of the documents on the floor. "There's nothing here!" she yelled. "We're wasting time."

Tamara's eyes went to the document that Sherry had angrily dropped. "Let me see that."

"See what?"

"The document you just dropped. Let me see it."

Though confused, Sherry gave the document to her anyway.

Tamara read through it very quickly, and then a small smile spread across her face. "I know where Rachel and Ben are holding my mother."

"What?" they chorused.

"Ben is holding my mother at this address." She held up the documents for them to see. "I'm going to call the police."

Joe took the document from her and then glanced back at her. "Wait, Tamara. This paper is for one of our warehouses. We sold it out about three months ago. Ben handled the sale. How can you be sure that's where he's holding your mom?"

With all urgency, she stood up from the floor. "Let's assume that you're the one handling the sale, and I'm the buyer. Now, I've just agreed to buy this warehouse. What happens next?"

He hesitated.

"C'mon, Joe, I'm trying to prove a point."

He shrugged. "Alright." Gesturing the armchair opposite of him, he said, "Go ahead and take a seat while we fill out the forms and close the deal."

Tamara did as she was told.

Taking out two forms from inside the drawer, Joe gave one to Tamara and kept one for himself. "Please, go ahead and fill out those forms, while I complete these." He took out a pen from the pocket of his suit jacket and began to fill out the forms.

"Can I have a pen please?" Tamara asked.

"Sure," he replied, pointing to the stack of pens right beside her at the edge of the table.

"Why didn't you give me your pen?"

He hesitated longer than a second. "Well, because I'm using it. I have to fill out this form..."

She cut him off. "Stop! That's what I'm getting at. See, these papers were both handled by Ben." She showed him the documents. "The ink looks the same. And like you just proved, Ben couldn't have given his own pen to the buyer because he would be using it at the same time."

Joe raised a brow. "What are you implying?"

"That Ben was the buyer and the seller."

Joe shook his head to disagree. "That's not possible. I mean, we weren't there, but Ben could have given the buyer his pen. They both could have used the same pen."

She glanced at Drake, seriously hoping he would agree with her.

"I want to side with you, Tamara, but a pen?" He shook his head. "Not enough."

She let out a deep breath and grabbed another documents from the stack on the floor. "This is the paper of another warehouse that was also sold by Connor Corp three months ago. It has the same square feet and space compared to the one that was sold by Ben. This warehouse was sold for 1.2 million dollars, and Ben sold this other warehouse for $25,000. I can't see any reason he would do that except that..."

Joe interrupted. "He was the buyer. Son of a bitch has been ripping off Connor Corp."

"So if he actually bought this warehouse for himself, I believe that's where he would hold my mother."

They all nodded in agreement.

Grabbing her cellphone, Tamara made a quick call.

"Detective Lance, I think I know where Ben Murray is holding my mom."

****

It was an abandoned warehouse. It has the CC logo boldly written on it, so he knew it was a Connor Corp facility. He glanced around and noticed everything was still. Silence covered the building like a graveyard.

Still glancing around, looking over his shoulder as if something was going to pounce on him. He walked carefully to the front door, but before he could open it, it opened by itself. He walked in slowly, and straight ahead was Mara's mom tied to a chair, lips sealed. His rescue instinct kicked in, and he tried running to cut her loose.

He hadn't gotten close enough when Ben stepped between them. "Not that easy, boy."

He stopped.

Before he could say anything to Ben, he heard a voice that he recognized so well.

"Hello, son."

He turned back to look at her, and there she stood, pointing a gun at him. All the while he had been running from Lisa, thinking she was the one who wanted him dead. Not in a thousand lifetimes would he have thought the traitor to be his mother or even Ben.

With the pain of betrayal burning hotly through him, he tried to say something to her. but he lacked the words. In some ways, this was worse than if it was Lisa or Joe that had been trying to kill him. Rachel was his mother. Mothers are supposed to love their children and protect them. But, Rachel only saw him as a means to an end.

"Let her go," he said, pointing to Mara's mom. "You want me, and you have me. I'll do anything you want."

"Of course you will," Rachel said.

And then Ben slowly led him to a table and a chair and gestured for him to sit.

Raymond gently did as he was told.

Ben lowered his gun, brought out a laptop and placed it on the table before Raymond.

"How much liquid cash does Connor Corp have right now?" Rachel asked.

Before he could reply, Ben interrupted. "And don't even think of lying. I have an estimate. I just don't know the right amount."

Raymond swallowed. "545 million dollars."

"Good," Ben replied. "You're going to transfer everything to a foreign account..."

Raymond frowned. "That's not even possible. That's too much money to transfer at one time. The bank won't let it go through."

"Of course they will."

Raymond's eyes went wide. "You got to my bank manager. too?"

Ben gave a knowing smile. "You will also transfer to me your controlling share of Connor Corp."

His palm became a fist as he scowled. "And if I don't?"

"She dies," Rachel replied, pointing her gun at Mara's mom. "And don't think for a second that I won't. You remember what happened to Dahlia, right?"

He took a deep breath, his fist getting tighter.

Ben must have noticed it. "Think twice, Raymond. Can your fist get to me faster than I'm able to pull the trigger?"

Raymond shook with impotent rage as he unclenched his fist.

"Son," Rachel said, modulating her voice to soothe like that voice mothers used to pacify a crying baby, "maybe you're thinking that her life is not worth everything that you're about to lose."

He glanced at Mara's mom. She gave a tearful shudder, shaking her head, her eyes pleading with him not to give it all up for her sake.

"But think about it. How will Mara feel if she finds out that you let her mother die just to hold on to your money and your position at Connor Corp?"

Rachel was right. He wasn't exactly doing this to save Mara's mom. He was doing it for Mara.

Raymond tried to calm himself. "You win," he admitted. "I will do everything you ask. But tell me, how you were able to pull this off?" He shook his head in disbelief. "I can't believe you did this. It was smart of you."

Rachel's face turned pleasant, the hint of a smile plastered on her face. "I couldn't have done this without Ben. Ben wanted Connor Corp, I wanted to be free, and I wanted a good life. So we became a team. It was easy for Ben to get Dahlia on. She was a greedy bitch, anyway. She was with Joe because of the Connor wealth, and when Ben told her that you were the heir, not Joe, it was easy to convince her to come after you and pass the pregnancy off as yours. And then we needed someone who knew exactly where you would be at a particular time. That was how we got Anita on board."

"Dahlia came after you, and I know men. They never can control that little man between their legs. So you fell for Dahlia's trap. And you fell for it again in Paris when Dahlia told you she was carrying your baby. You married her. I knew you would. You had a rough childhood and wouldn't want the same for your child."

Raymond cut in. "You tricked me into marrying Dahlia? Why? What's the plan?"

"The plan was for Dahlia to watch your every move and get close enough to kill you. And when

you were dead, Ben was to take over at Connor
Corp since he was the next in command. Dahlia fed
you the arsenic and you started getting sick. Dahlia
told us about your visit to the hospital, and that was
why we told Dr. Morgan to give an incorrect diag-
nosis. Everybody can be bought, Raymond. You
only have to find out their price. For Dr. Morgan,
it's $100,000."

"Dahlia was working for you. So why did you
kill her?"

"She was talking. We needed to shut her up before she started calling names."

Raymond let out a deep breath and lowered his
head. When he brought his head back up, hot tears
filled his eyes, but he didn't shed them. "Why are
you doing this? You're my mother."

She lowered herself and brought her face close
to his. "Now that's not exactly true."

His brow pulled together in a confusing frown,
his heart racing in anticipation.

A grin spread across her face. "You didn't
know?"

"Know what?" Raymond yelled. And then he
tried to calm his voice. "Know what? You're going
to kill me anyway. Don't I at least deserve to know
the truth?"

She nodded slowly. "Very well then," she replied. "I was working for Connors," she began.
"And once in a while my little sister, Rita, would
come around to spend time with me at work. I
didn't know that James Connor was screwing my
sister. It took me such a long time to find out. And
then Rita got pregnant with you and died while

trying to have you. I was her only relative. So I adopted you. For years, I raised you. I tried to let James take full responsibility for you, but he wouldn't, because he was scared of his wife. He was so afraid of Lisa and wasn't man enough to stand up to his responsibilities. And that was why I did what I did. Everything I did, I did for you, but instead, you stood as a witness against me."

"Everything you did, you did for yourself!" he yelled. "I spoke to James on his deathbed. He told me how you blackmailed him and took a lot of money from him. When he refused to pay you any further, you tried to kill him."

She stiffened, her back straight. Putting the gun closer to Raymond's head, she said, "Talk time is over, son."

Raymond scowled. "You won't get away with it. The police will hunt you. They will find you."

"I doubt that. Before the police know what is happening, your 545 million dollars and I will be in Morocco, where they can't get to me. And I'll be living out my Casablanca fantasy."

"Okay, enough!" Ben yelled with a hint of urgency in his voice. "Let's start by transferring your controlling shares to me. I've had my lawyers draft some papers," he said, pointing to a folder on the screen.

Raymond slowly leaned closer to the laptop to click over the folder Ben had pointed to.

Suddenly, the sound of police siren swallowed up the silence that had once covered the warehouse.

"They know we're here!" Rachel said urgently as Ben reached for the ammunition and loaded up his gun, just as she had done shortly before.

"Don't you think I know that?" he snapped angrily. "Listen, as long as we stay close to him…" he gestured roughly to Raymond, "…we've got nothing to worry about. Stay calm and keep a cool head. Don't respond to anything they say unless they're talking terms, understand?"

Rachel nodded curtly and kept her gun pointed at Raymond, but halfway between her own torso and his head so she could pistol-whip anyone should they manage to get in close quarters. An intense silence stole over the warehouse in which they had taken refuge, each one of the pair looking around for the smallest sign of motion and straining their ears for the faintest sound. Raymond, helpless and immobile in his current state, did nothing but close his eyes and try to formulate a plan of his own. There wasn't much he could do, but the smallest effort might make the difference he needed.

A dull *boom* permeated the silence, as though something loud had been slammed in the distance. Ben and Rachel immediately tensed and crouched, taking cover behind the metallic shelves that created aisles throughout the dismal warehouse, as though it were some long-forsaken supermarket. Ever-louder booms, increasing in frequency, continued to break the silence as the sound of many approaching footsteps clattered in their direction. Rachel rested her hands on the shelf in front of her, clearing away a few items to create a line of sight as she took aim at the door.

The halls beyond the warehouse door grew quiet for a moment, as if the intensity in the room was a viscous liquid, Ben slowly and carefully moved his hands toward Raymond until the gun was poised toward his head.

The thunderous kick upon the doors was deafening.

As though chain and lock meant nothing, the doors parted swiftly to either side and barely re-mained on their hinges as a platoon of ten officers ran in and took in the view in front of them—rows and rows of metallic shelves spread across the room, creating a number of narrow aisles between them. At the end of the centermost aisle, right in front of the doors through which the police had entered, was the kneeling form of a now bound Raymond.

Noticing him, an officer made to go and free him, but was stopped by the outraised hand of his colleague. "Ben Murray and Rachel Brock, you're hereby under arrest for the murder of Dahlia Con-nor and the kidnapping of Mrs. Stephanie Price." Upon hearing his voice, the others took notice of two forms hidden behind the shelves on either side of the hostages and quickly took aim, in case they had to return fire.

"Under arrest, huh?" Ben asked smoothly. "What a comfort that would be to our good friend Raymond here, especially after he's dead. Do you really think you've got a hand to play here, officer?"

The man that had once tried to free Raymond put down his gun as a symbol of peace and moved forward, his hands raised pacifically. "There's nothing left for you to do here. You're surrounded. If you surrender peacefully, you won't have to be charged with resisting arrest and assaulting police officers with deadly force."

Rachel, who had been quietly suppressing her neuroses until now, spoke in the shaky voice of a woman about to burst, no longer able to control her emotions. "Not another step closer."

The man paused his advance for a second, and then continued. "I just want to…"

"NOT ANOTHER STEP CLOSER!" Rachel shrieked, impulsively pulling the trigger and shooting the man dead. At once, chaos erupted before the man even hit the floor.

Ben swore shortly before changing his own aim and adding his gunfire to the cacophony of zinging bullets as they narrowly missed and clanged against the shelves. The remaining nine officers loosed their fire upon Ben and Rachel's approximate positions, careful to aim away from Raymond's body which had fallen forward upon his face at the torrential sounds of gunshots.

Rachel continued to run across the back of the warehouse, taking cover behind the shelves and wildly loosing shots between the aisles without regard for aim, whereas Ben shrewdly took his time switching between shelves for cover and periodically aiming back to fire. In an attempt to gain ground, some of the offers had broken formation and walked across the sides in an attempt to circumvent the shelves.

They're trying to outflank us, Ben realized, gritting his teeth. Within a few moments, men would appear on either side now, and they'd have a clear shot at him. Time was of the essence, and he was quickly running out. In hasty urgency, he looked wildly toward Raymond's form, only to be shocked when it wasn't there.

Seeing his chance shortly after the exchange began, Raymond did what he could to squirm down the aisle. He'd only managed to move a foot when Ben practically sprung upon him. "NO!" Ben snarled viciously, converging upon Raymond.

It had gone relatively silent as Ben pounced on Raymond, but now a single shot shattered the silence, following by a pained cry as Ben ended up sprawled on the ground next to his hostage, blood pouring from a wound in his arm. "Rachel..." he called out desperately as he made a pathetic attempt to get his gun, well out of reach.

Initially shocked that Ben had been wounded, Rachel snapped out of her frantic demeanor and quickly took aim for Raymond's head just as the officers aimed at hers. "Checkmate." She sneered devilishly. "Drop the guns or else."

Another blast–solitary, like the first– penetrated the air. The sneer never left her face, not even as she crumpled and hit the floor with a solid *thump.*

"You are under arrest for the kidnapping of Raymond Connor," the officer standing behind Ben declared solemnly.

Raymond gradually stood up and glanced at the body of his mother lying lifelessly on the floor. *The battle is over*, he thought as he let out a deep breath of relief.

EPILOGUE

One thing Tamara liked about her new office building was that it was right across from the Connor Corp building. She could see Raymond very easily and anytime she wanted. And even better, she could see the windows of Raymond's office from her own.

But as she stood at the window this night, looking at Raymond's office, she felt uneasy. Everything looked peaceful. There was no sign that Raymond was there. She saw no reflection of light or silhouette of him.

Raymond said he would be working late into the night. Had he lie to her or did something happen to him?

Walking back to her desk, she grabbed her cellphone and called Raymond. It rang and rang, but he didn't pick up.

Was he okay? If he had a change of plans, he would have called to let her know. It was so unlike Raymond. Her uneasiness increased with each passing second, but then she tried to calm herself and not think the worst. Maybe he had an urgent meeting somewhere and couldn't get to his phone.

The moment passed and her cellphone rang. She pressed the green button.

"Ray, where have you been?" She tried not to sound too worried, but it was still evident in her voice.

"Right about now, a limo should be waiting for you outside your office building."

"What?" she said, walking to her window to see things for herself. When she peeped through the window, the headlights flashed at her.

"What is this, Ray? What kind of game are you playing?"

"The limo driver has a package for you. In this package is a dress, shoes and purse to match. Get dressed and hop in."

"But where is he taking me?"

"Trust me, Mara," he replied.

"Okay. I trust you. But I've been worried sick about you. Where are you?"

"Vegas, baby," he replied, a smile in his voice, and then he hung up.

She went outside and took the package from the limo driver. When she got back in the building, she opened the huge white box. Inside was red dress perfectly folded into a square. She took it out, itching to try it on.

In the twinkling of an eye, she was in the dress. She fixed her makeup and was ready to go.

The limo driver held the door open for her, and she hopped in. The drive to the airport was quiet and short. She didn't know why, but her heart was beating fast, racing. She tried to calm her nerves. She wasn't a lamb about to be taken to slaughter.

She was going to Vegas, that much she knew by now. But still, Raymond should have given her fair warning beforehand so she could plan things and clear the load of work on her desk.

When they got to the airport, the crew led her away from the commercial terminals. As they led her to the FBO, she knew she was flying Lily.

It was a five hours flight from Baltimore to Vegas. Tamara would have died of boredom if she wasn't already dying of anxiousness.

After landing at the airport, another limo came for her. As she sat in the back, all she could think about was what to say to Raymond. She wasn't some kind of servant he could just summon anytime and anyway he wanted. Whatever happened to Baby, you want to come with me to Vegas? They should have traveled together, not separately.

The limo parked, and she freshened up her make-up before stepping out. But when she did, she glanced around. Something just hinted to her that she had been here before. The place felt very familiar.

And then she looked closely, right in front of her, the Palms Place Hotel boldly written on the beautiful building. That was it. The Palms Place Hotel. She had definitely been here before.

It was as if everyone working at the hotel was expecting her. They welcomed her, while she managed to maintain a steady smile on her face. Two bellhops led her to another part of the building. She wanted to ask where, but Raymond said to trust him, so she just followed, no questions asked, like a lamb about to be slaughtered.

And then the door opened. The bellhops stopped, smiled and gestured for her to go in as if to say, *Very well, miss, we can't go beyond here.*

Slowly, she walked into the room. It was dark, and Tamara could see nothing. She knew this was some kind of prank Raymond was playing, but she didn't know what to expect. Her heart raced in anticipation.

And then she saw candlelight at the far left of the room. She walked toward the light, and as she got closer, she saw Raymond and felt calm surge through her.

Only a few steps away from the table, Raymond stood and walked toward her. Circling her arms around his neck, she hugged him before asking, "What is this, Ray?"

"I had urgent business in Vegas." His voice was low. "We made plenty of memories here, so I thought it would be good if it's you and me here again."

She nodded and smiled.

She had a whole speech rehearsed in her mind about how it was so wrong for him to just summon her like that, without any notice. But seeing him, right now, she melted, smiling like a teenage girl on a date for the first time. As he took her hands, she felt his gaze move over her, and from the look on his face, she knew he liked what he saw. "You look… delicious."

She smiled. "You look yummy, too."

He gently led her to the table, held the chair for her and helped her sit. And then he went back to sit opposite of her. The candle on the table was small, only enough to light up their table.

Raymond had ordered their meal. She kept talking and talking about her trip to Vegas as they ate. Grabbing the flute of champagne on her side of the table, she took a sip. When she lowered the glass, she saw Raymond bring out a small black box from the pocket of his suit jacket.

Such a fool she had been! Sending a limo to get her. Letting her fly Lily. Bringing her back to the Palms Place Hotel where it all started. She should have figured it out.

Tears gathered in her eyes.

"Mara," his voice was low and gentle. "I not only break your heart, I shattered it. And you forgave my foolishness and took me back. That is something no other woman would do." He paused and swallowed hard, the candlelight dancing in his brown eyes. "Everything I am today is because of you. You fought for me, fought my battles as if they were yours. You believed in me; you had faith in me; you gave me your commitment; you gave me your all; you loved me with so much love that sometimes I think I don't deserve you. And God knows I love you, too. I love you so, so much that sometimes I feel like I need an extra heart to hold it all. And I can't picture the rest of my life without you by my side." He paused and let out a deep breath. Slowly he held the 15-carat diamond ring in his hand and went down on one knee. "Tamara Price, will you do me the honor of marrying me?"

She sat there, tears streaming down her cheeks. She swallowed hard, staring deep into his eyes, and she knew all the love in those brown eyes was for her. "Yes," she said. She held out her left hand for him, smiling amid sobs. "Yes, I'll marry you."

Sliding the ring down her fourth finger, he rose to his feet and held her in his arms. "Thank you. Thank you, Mara." He kissed her lips, her cheek, her neck.

And then Tamara heard the sound of people clapping their hands and the light went on.

Her eyes went wide.

Drake, Joe, Sherry, Megan, her mom and some other people she couldn't recognize because of the buzz in her head at the moment.

She smiled and glanced at Raymond. "They've been here all the while."

He smiled back and shrugged.

She smiled and her smile turned into laughs as they hugged her, congratulating her on the engagement.

They partied into the night.

It was well past midnight when Tamara and Raymond retired into their room. As she entered the room, it felt familiar. She knew it was the same room they had used the last time they were here. Raymond must have gone through a lot to get them that same room again. Memories of what they had done in this room came back to her, and she glanced at Raymond, smiling. "Kiss me," she said softly. Slipping his shirt to the floor, she unbuttoned his pants and pulled him free, holding him in her soft, gentle hands.

He slipped his hands to her waist, quickly lifting her off the floor, his hands underneath her bottom. His lips kissed her passionately. Wet and glistening, her body warming, the goose bumps dissolving into the night air. He kissed her like she'd never been kissed before. His strong muscular arms wrapped around her waist and lifted her, turning her in the same action and laying her down on the bed, his now naked body on top of hers. She knew this was it. And her entire soul fizzed like lemonade escaping from a bottle. He made her glow like no other man could. She lived in his bright brown eyes. He looked back at her with a smile afforded to a man who was madly in love with his woman. He could not contain his eagerness as he lifted her knees and entered her softly. She moaned and purred under his control, his heavy body pressing her down, holding her onto the sheets as he thrust inside her, harder and harder, watching the delight and ecstasy in her eyes as he shifted her body with every motion. His arms holding her tight, his lips all over hers. Hands roaming up and down her soft, sensuous skin, glistening with sweat and the sweet, sickly candy taste of sex. She yanked his head back and bit her lip for him. Wanting more, wanting it harder. "Please, baby... please," she cried as he licked her neck, moaning into her ear as their bodies writhed and twisted into each other as they climaxed together. His breath was taken from him just as much as hers. Sweat-covered and exhausted, he slid to her side, holding her hand firm. He slipped her under the covers and lay with her, his arms her pillow, her hair his comforter.

AFTERWORD

Thank you to everyone who left a review on amazon for *When Love Hurts*. If you enjoyed reading *I Choose You*, would you mind leaving a review for it, too, on amazon? Good reviews really help sell books, so if you don't mind, I'd be forever grateful.

And thank you so much for continuing on this love trip with Raymond and Tamara. Fortunately, we haven't seen the last of them. I've decided to write a prequel to take you to the beginning of their love and show you how it all started.

I'm going to have the prequel out as soon as I can, but before that, I have another new book that will be published soon enough. Be on the lookout for *I'm a Gold Digger*. On the next few pages, you will find a brief excerpt from it.

Thank you again for your support.

Aderonke Moyinlorun

Facebook: @AderonkeMoyinlorun

Twitter: @IAmAderonke

Website: www.authoraderonke.com

SPECIAL SNEEK PREVIEW

On the following pages you will find a brief excerpt from

I'm

a

Gold Digger

<u>ONE</u>

I'm writing this because I want to change, because I've lost everything, because I'm heartbroken, because I'm in love, and because I have learned that money, wealth and riches can never equal love.

And even though I hate myself for what I did, I can only hope that I get another chance to love him right...

****

Okay, I'm sorry for getting emotional on you. I'm really not that kind of girl, I swear. My name is Eva Perry, and I'm a gold digger. Yes, a very competent and professional gold digger.

I'm not talking about digging gold in South African mines. I'm talking about dating rich men just to have a share of their money.

I'm 24 years old and I've been married twice. My first marriage happened in a lavish and expensive wedding when I was 22. My marriage to the millionaire ended just three months after. I made life unbearable for my husband. He asked for divorce, and I walked away with a very fat bank account. I'm talking millions of dollars.

OH! Did I mention properties, too?

I walked away with quite a lot of properties. I own a home in Miami, Florida, and another in Los Angeles — and so many other properties around the world.

I'm going to stop boasting about my assets!

My second marriage happened seven months after the first. Unlike the first, this marriage lasted a bit longer. It lasted a whopping one year! The man was difficult. After everything I did to make him miserable, he wouldn't ask for a divorce. He was so greedy that he was afraid of losing his wealth to me. Come on! He married me! I have the right to his wealth as much as he does.

Anyways, despite all his efforts, I won. I always do. The marriage ended, and I walked away with a lot of wealth.

I was looking for the next victim when I met him. He was the only one that made me feel different. Fall in love. Entirely. Over and over again.

But we'll get to that soon enough.

By now, you probably think I'm a heartless bitch that deserves what I get, but wait till you hear the whole story. I wasn't always like this. I wasn't always heartless. So, I'm going to take you back to the beginning.